Mystery in Ulster County

RICHARD HORVATH

First Edition

Fulton Books, Inc.
Meadville, PA

Published by Fulton Books 2021

ISBN 978-1-63710-051-6 (paperback)
ISBN 978-1-63710-052-3 (digital)

Printed in the United States of America

It was 11:00 p.m. on a Friday night. I had just ordered the tastiest bacon cheeseburger you will ever introduce to your taste buds. I looked across the table at the most beautiful woman you will ever set eyes on. I started to open my mouth when the call came. It was my first night off in nine days. The third attempt of a date with Nicole, and we were doing fine until the call.

"Mecelli, yeah, where, okay." Another woman. I thought about the other two; the reasons my other dates get cut short. Before I knew it, Nicole was standing and putting her coat on. I knew at that moment it was the last date.

As I was headed to the Gully Road, my mind was racing. The third woman in as many months, wondering if anything was left behind this time. As I pulled up to the scene, my partner, Anthony LaFonte, was by the victim.

Detective LaFonte was new to homicide—seven months in the department. He served on patrol for two years while studying forensics and crime scenes. He was on his way to becoming a crime scene investigator, then decided on homicide. I took him under my wing. His mother left when he was eight years old, and his father took it out on him. "Hey, Tone, what do we have?" he asked as I was walking over. I saw her lying there, arms and legs spread, mutilation in the vagina area, and red lipstick drawn like a clown's smile. I knew, at that moment, it was the third victim. Tone turned to me, holding the victim's purse. Floodlights were set up. It looked like 11:30 a.m., the way you could see all around the area.

CSI was scouring the area. John Grimes was the lead investigator. I scoped him out. "Hey, John," I said as I navigated around the scene.

"Hey, Joe." We talked for a while, and I left with no more than I started with. I walked back to where the body was.

The coroner was just zipping the bag. "Hey, Peter." Peter Fortier was a big man, mid-forties, and gray beyond his years. We talked about the body the same as the two crime scenes before. The only thing left was a lipstick tube, the same thing. We made plans to meet at Hot Shotz later that evening.

Over the years, John, Peter, and I became friends. We meet occasionally at a local bar and grill in Kerhonkson called Hot Shotz. The food is delicious, and the atmosphere is relaxing. It was 3:30 a.m., time to get some sleep.

Tone and I pulled up at the same time; we both had coffee and egg sandwiches. It was 9:00 a.m. on Saturday morning. We went in, put our notes together, and added the victims, pictures, and information to the board.

The first victim, Mary Lynne Spiel: a White female, twenty-seven years old, worked at the local Shoprite, had long straight blond hair, and always pulled up in a ponytail. She was five feet, two inches tall with a medium build. She was single, no kids, and no steady man or woman. According to her friends and family, she was a good and honest person. Her investigation was hitting a dead end.

The second victim, Natasha Anne Brown: African American female, thirty-four years old, divorced, no kids, no current boyfriend, short black hair, five feet, seven inches tall, medium build, and worked at Kohl's by Wurtsboro. Her divorce was normal—belongings were split. The house and car went to her. Her ex ended up with practically nothing. We interviewed her ex-husband, Joe. He really didn't have hard feelings and moved to Virginia, where he was offered a job two years before the murder and never came back. With no other leads, the case slowed.

Now victim number three, twenty-one-year-old Elisabeth Frances Coker. According to her driver's license, she lived at 5 Church Street, Apartment 3, Ellenville, New York. After the search of her apartment, we found she was a vegetarian and had a cat. We found a registration renewal for a Chevy Malibu, a green four-door, and that she was a messy housekeeper. We searched for her car, but it was not there. According to her neighbors, she liked to party and had all kinds of people coming and going at all times of the day and night. Her downstairs neighbor, a gossipy old lady who owned the house, was getting ready to evict her. Her rent was always paid on time, but the noise and the goings-on were too much for her to bear. She had insisted we sit for tea while she told us about Liz as she called her. After two hours, old lady Griz's life store, we left with a couple of names and a place to avoid unless you had absolutely nothing to do for an afternoon or so.

It was 6:20 p.m., and Tone, John, Peter, and I were at Hot Shotz ordering the best bacon cheeseburgers and fries you ever want to eat.

My mind wandered to Nicole, where the night before we were seated at the same table. I really liked Nicole. We met at the doctor's office where she was the head nurse, and I was a patient. She was thirty-eight years old but looked like twenty-eight. I really enjoyed being around her. I was hoping we could have a nice long relationship.

My mind came back to Hot Shotz; everyone was looking at me. Tone said, "What do you think, Joe?"

I apologized and asked them, "What do I think about what?"

He repeated, with attitude, "We have three women—different races, age, hair, height, build, and different walks of life. Do you think it could be different subjects copying each other?"

I replied, "No, I don't think so."

"Why not?" Tone quickly answered, "The fact that the knife that was used to mutilate the women's groin areas were left at each scene wiped spotless and the lipsticks that were used also left and wiped spotless. But if we find the suspects, maybe we would find they have a knife missing, and they had an excess amount of red lipstick."

John interrupted, "First, the knives that were left at the scenes were a cheap run of the mill made in China, a steak knife that you can buy anywhere in either a set or single. Secondly, all the red lipstick is the same made in China that you could get in any dollar or discount store."

"Third," I said, "the knife and lipstick left at the scene were not released to the public."

Peter added after our meals and fresh mugs arrived, "There is a certain way the mutilation was done. It would never hit the papers."

With little conversation, we were enjoying our meals too much to spoil it with a talk. As soon as our plates were empty, Tone started with, "It doesn't have to hit the papers for everyone to know. These things are happening in Ellenville. It's such a small town. You could do something on one side of town, and by the time you get to the other side, people already know about it."

He is right, I thought. Ellenville, a village, used to be a place that employed a thousand plus people, but with the closing of Schrade Knives and then VAW Aluminum, people here stayed closer to home after work, and most people have nothing better to do than worry about what other people do.

"But still," John said, "the women were found later in the evening, and I am sure they didn't notice exactly what was left at the scene, and even if they did see something, the horror of the way the bodies were left, it probably didn't even register."

I started to speak when I noticed everyone looking at me, not above me. They had a look on their faces of teenagers looking at the girls' cheerleading team. Then I smelled a familiar fragrance, and a smile hit my face—Nicole.

"Joe, could I please talk to you a minute?" I jumped up and walked outside. I got to the door and turned around, and every man and some women were staring seriously at me. I gave them a smile and walked out of the bar.

"Joe," she began, "I have to say this while I have the courage. I really enjoy talking and spending time with you. I know we had an attempt at three different dates and all three were cut short, but I think about you all the time, and I want this to work out." I wanted to tell her she was on my mind a lot, and I wanted nothing more than to spend the rest of my life with her. Instead, we were embraced in a kiss that made me feel like every muscle in my body was like Jell-O. We ended up at her house, down the road off 209, as it was closer. It was a night unlike any I've experienced. The sex was hot and out of this world, as if I died and went to Heaven.

The ringing was bringing me back to reality. I awoke; the aroma of fresh coffee and bacon brought on a smile.

"Mecelli."

"Oh, what's up, Tone? Yeah, well, I'm sorry. Yeah, I'll be there in an hour."

I found the kitchen. "It wasn't a dream," I said.

Nicole turned, looked at me with a smile, and said, "No, but it's a dream come true." As I wrapped my arms around her, I felt the weird feeling I felt when I was fifteen and had my first crush. I should have been out on my morning run. At forty-one, I run three miles every day and work out a few times a week, but this morning, I sat and enjoyed breakfast with Nicole. It was an hour past when I told Tone I would meet him. With Nicole, I felt warm and safe, unlike any other relationship I've been in. I enjoyed talking with her. I have never discussed a case with any woman I had been with, but Nicole was different, and that's why I was an hour late.

"Hey, Tone. What's up?"

"Joe," he said, trying to hide the fact that he was furious, "you told me you would be here an hour ago."

"All right, I'm sorry. I got held up, next time I'll call, okay?"

"Okay," he said, plopping down in his chair.

"Who do you want to see first?" I asked.

"While I was waiting an hour for you, I took it upon myself to go pick up Tom Sherpa," he said. Tom Sherpa was first on the list from old lady Griz.

I said, "Tom Sherpa, my name is Detective Joe Mecelli, and this is my partner Detective Anthony LaFonte. We need to ask you some questions about Elizabeth Coker. First, I would like to let you know you are not under arrest, and you have the right not to talk to us, understand."

Tom asked, "Yes?"

I said, "We have a few questions. Do you mind answering?"

Tom answered, "Sure."

"Okay, how do you know Elizabeth?"

"We knew each other from school."

"Are you her boyfriend?"

He laughed, "No."

"Why is that funny?"

"Liz don't like boys if you know what I mean."

"Yeah, I know what you mean. Mrs. Griz, Elizabeth's landlord, said you go there a lot at different times of day and night, why is that." No answer. I thought a moment and told him I was not interested in any activities except for the homicide, so whatever he told me, he would not get in trouble from me.

"Okay," he said, "I go there for the parties and to buy some weed."

"Does she sell anything other than weed?"

"Yeah, but I only smoke a little weed now and then. I don't do anything else."

"What else does she deal?"

"Coke and ecstasy."

"Were you there last night?"

"Yeah."

"What time?"

"Around seven."

"Was anyone there?"

"Only Liz. She said she was going out."

"Did she say where?"

"No."

"What did you do when you left?"

"I went to my parents in Kingston."

"What time did you get home?"

"I left there around midnight, so probably one."

"What's your father's address?"

He gave the address and left. I placed a call to the Sheriff's Office in Kingston. The father said Tom came over around 7:30 p.m. for the mother's birthday party and left around midnight. He worked at the local Stewart's Shop and worked his shift of twelve to seven but left five minutes early, and the father said he showed up with his Stewart's shirt on, and we had to eliminate him. In the next few days, we went down the list, and like Tom, everyone was eliminated.

I was seeing Nicole from time to time, and we set up a nice night. On my way there, I got a call from Peter. He and John were stopping at Hot Shotz and asked if I would like to stop. "Sure," I said. I was two and a half hours early going to Nicole's, so I called Tone. "Tone," I said, "we are meeting at Hot Shotz."

"I'll be right there," he said. Tone is like a son to me, being twenty-three and new to homicide. I started inviting him everywhere I went, except to Nicole's. Once we got to Hot Shotz, we started going over the cases. Everything about them was so similar, but the women were so different. I looked at my watch; it's 4:48 p.m. I was meeting Nicole at five, so I drank down my beer and told the guys I had to meet Nicole.

They all laughed and kidded with me, except Tone. He explained they had three-like murders, and he needed me to work harder with him, for he was too new to do things on his own. I told him to kick back tonight, and for the next few days, they would work the cases all day and night if he wanted. He was grumbling as I left.

Nicole and I had a wonderful night. Dinner at the White Wolf on 209, a movie in Kingston, and my place for a nightcap and a little piece of heaven. I was woken from a much-needed sleep. Between my heavy caseload and my night with Nicole, I was drained.

"Mecelli?"

"Yeah, where, I'll be right there."

As I came out of the bathroom, Nicole met me with a hot cup of coffee mug. "Another one?" she asked. I nodded my head, wondering what I ever did to deserve someone like her. She hugged me tight, kissed me, and said, "Call me," as she went back to bed. I wanted to follow her but left the house.

It was 2:30 a.m. when I pulled on to Berme Road off Port Ben. There were two NYS trooper cars. They had the road blocked. I asked who found her, and he motioned to another trooper who was talking to a middle-aged man, a Mr. Fider. "He has trouble sleeping sometimes. He walks his dog."

I walked over to Mr. Fider, "Hi, I'm Detective Mecelli. Mind if I talk to you?"

"Sure."

"Come, let's sit in my car. Mr. Fider, could you explain how you found the body?"

"Sure, I have trouble sleeping, so I walked my dog for a while. Well, tonight, he ran into the weeds here a few feet from the road and started barking. I shined my flashlight and saw this young lady lying there. I called 911."

"Did you see any cars around?"

"No, I don't usually see any this time of the night."

By the end of my interview with Mr. Fider, the scene was lit up. Peter was checking out the body, John and his crew were scouring the area, and Tone was going through a purse. I walked over and talked to John. He wanted to know how my night went. I told him another time. He said they found the same as the other three—cheap knife and red lipstick, both wiped clean. No tire tracks. Due to the growth, no footprints. As I walked over toward the body, Peter said, "There's the big stud." Tone looked at me but said nothing.

"What do you think?" I asked Peter.

"Same lipstick, smile, same mutilation."

Shit, I thought. We haven't even finished with number three, and now we have number four.

Back at the station, Tone finally spoke, "How's Nicole? Still seeing her?"

Hearing her name reminded me of how she had a hot cup of coffee ready for me before I left and how I enjoyed every drop. I replied, "She is fine, and yes, I am still seeing her."

Tone asked, "She's not upset that every time you are together, it gets cut short?"

That's a weird question, I thought, but it goes with the job of a homicide detective. "No," I said, "she made me coffee before I left this morning." The way she looked in one of those shirts. Tone cleared his throat. I was brought back to work mode. I had to call in and get more help. Tone went into the shop, as we call it, while I made the call. I walked into the shop and smelled coffee brewing, and Tone was hanging the fourth photo on the wall. They were sending two detectives. They would be here in a few hours. We went through the purse of our fourth victim, Lucia Onya Lopez, forty-two years old, and lives on High Street in Napanoch. We had just finished adding her information on the board when our help arrived.

"Detective Mecelli?"

"Hi, I'm Detective Gary Banks, and this is my partner Detective Lucy Pinia."

"Hi, I'm Detective Joe Mecelli, and this is Det. Anthony LaFonte. Call me Joe," I said as we shook hands and got to know each other in a five-minute conversation. I realized that Tone was interrupting the questions asked to me with his answers. He was nervous. I thought Gary was in homicide for seven years, Lucy for four years, myself for eleven years, and Tone for only eight months now. Gary started his career in Buffalo where I had grown up and was glad to be away. I didn't mind snow and cold winters, but Buffalo was a little much for me. I moved to Accord when I was twenty-two and have been here ever since.

Over fresh coffee, we started with our first victim, Mary Lynn Spiel, found on Fordemoore Road under a bridge by a night fisherman. We went over our notes and interviews and how we had busted all leads in that case. Gary said he will take the file, read it over, and followed up.

We moved on to the second victim, Natasha Ann Brown, found up near Sam's Point area by a young couple looking for a place to, well, fool around, so to speak. We went over the information note and interviews, and that went to Lucy.

Now our third victim, Elizabeth Frances Coker. We were not quite done with leads when our fourth victim was found.

Victim four: Lucia Onya Lopez, forty-two years old, Puerto Rican, very pretty, and had a very nice shape for a forty-two-year-old. We were headed to her house to see what we could find.

Lucy said, "Okay, you guys go there. Me and Gary will take our files, go through them, and we will meet here in the morning."

"Sounds great," I said, then we left.

On the way to Lucia's house, Tone asked, "Do you think they will find something we didn't?"

I said, "You never know. Sometimes all it takes is a fresh set of eyes and a different train of thought." He grew quiet. We got to Lucia's house, and a neighbor was washing her car on one side and another was watering the flowers. Tone chose the flower lady, and I went to the car wash lady.

"Hi. I'm Detective Mecelli. I was wondering if I can ask a few questions about Ms. Lopez."

"Is she in trouble?" she asked. I told her no. The car wash lady turned out to be Sally Viconowski. She told me that Lucia went through a divorce last year and moved across the street with her mother.

I thanked her and went over and met Tone in front of the house. At the same time, we said she lived there with her mother. I had far too much experience in breaking people's hearts and turning their lives upside down, so I told Tone it was his turn. We knocked on the door, and a small, frail little woman of about seventy answered the door. As I stepped back, Tone walked in.

"Hello, Ma'am, my name is Detective Anthony LaFonte, and this is my partner Detective Joe Mecelli. May we come in and have a word?"

"What is this about," the senior Mrs. Lopez asked. Tone asked her if she had a daughter by the name of Lucia Onya Lopez.

She started to shake a little, and her voice got weak, "Yes, is she okay?" My partner pulled her driver's license out and asked if that was her. Mrs. Lopez looked at the license, tears started to roll down her cheeks. "Yes, where did you get this? Where is Lucy?"

"I'm very sorry," Tone said in a voice so sympathetic, you would think he had done this a thousand times. He put a hand on her shoulder and explained very softly how they had found her body last night, leaving out all the gruesome details and how they will not rest till they find the person responsible. He offered to call some family members to come be with her. He made some calls and sat with her while I went through Lucia's room. There was nothing there for me to investigate, except a picture of Lucia and a man standing on a beach. I left the room with the picture. Lucia's cousin was there when I walked out. I asked her to come into the kitchen with me. Her name was Carmen. I asked Carmen who the man in the photo was, and she said it was Lucia's new boyfriend. They had been seeing each other for a couple of months. I asked her if I could take the photo and promised to bring it back. We finished at Mrs. Lopez's house.

I said, "How about lunch? It is 11:15 a.m., and I am starving."

"Sure, where at?"

"How about Il Paradiso's?"

He looked at me and said, "You want to see Nicole, don't you?"

"Well, it's lunchtime, and she works close by," so I said. "Why, don't you like her? You don't even know her."

"You're right, I don't know her. Fine, let's go."

I called Nicole and set it up. When we got there, she was already sitting. She stood, and I thought about the naughty nurses on some videos I have seen and smiled. "Hello, Nic," I said as I hugged and kissed her.

"Hello, Anthony."

"Hi, Nicole." We ordered lunch, and Nicole asked Tone how I was treating him.

"Joe treats me just fine. He teaches me a lot, and I love working with him. Sometimes I get mad at him, but it's my fault really," he said with a chuckle.

After lunch, I told Nicole we would be working a lot and didn't know when I would have time to spend with her. She just smiled and said to at least call.

We went to the Bank of America to interview Lucia's coworkers, which only led us to Lucia's car. I called and had John tow the car and check it out. I received a call from Peter. He was done, same as the others, he said.

We located her boyfriend, Manny Guttierez. He worked for a local builder and broke down in tears at the news of Lucia. We took Manny back to the station. "We just need to ask a few questions if you are up to it."

"Yes, I'll be okay. I want to help all I can." I motioned to Tone, he looked at me, and I shook my head. Tone asked if he knew anyone who might do this.

Manny thought for a minute, and his jaw tightened, "I bet that bastard Mickey did it."

"Who is Mickey?" Tone asked.

"Miguel Nunez," Manny said, "that's Lucia's ex-husband."

"Where were you last night?" Manny looked at Tone like he wanted to tear his head off and then calmed.

"I worked my second job last night. Three nights a week, I work at the hospital cleaning. Can I go now? I would like to be with Lucia's family."

"Sure," Tone said and added, "I am truly sorry." We checked with the local builder. Manny is a hard worker. He worked at seven to three, never issues a day. We checked the hospital. Yes, he worked his four to twelve shift and had to stay late last night as a water main broke. He was there until 3:15 a.m. cleaning up.

We located Mickey and brought him in. Tone also handled this one. Miguel Nunez is a nice, polite man—hard to believe she left him. Tone started with why they divorced. He wanted to have kids; she didn't. They just drifted apart. He had an affair, she got pregnant, they moved in together.

"Where were you last night?

"Home all night? Yes. Nancy and I got a sitter, and we had a night to ourselves."

"Do you know anyone who might want to hurt Lucia?"

"No, she is a very nice lady. Everyone loved her." He checked out—off the list.

Tone and I went to Hot Shotz and went over some theories. At 2:00 a.m., we went home. We were in the shop by 9:00 a.m. Gary and Lucy came in at 9:15 a.m. Gary started, "I went over the files on Mary and reinterviewed a few friends. Mary was a member of Curves, a gym for women on Canal Street. I was going over today to ask some questions. Other than that, I came up with nothing."

Lucy said that Natasha was also a member of Curves, and that was all she came up with that wasn't in the notes. Tone was excited as maybe there was a connection there. I would also find out if Elizabeth and Lucia were also members. I told Gary and Lucy to follow up and let me know and told Tone we needed to get on Elizabeth's case. Gary and Lucy left. We pulled out Elizabeth's cell phone, thinking that we never found a family member for Elizabeth. I found a number that said "Mom." I called the number and got her address. We pulled into Mrs. Coker's driveway on Ulster Heights Road and went to the door. "You're up, Tone."

"Mrs. Coker?"

"Yes."

"I'm Detective Anthony LaFonte, and this is Detective Mecelli. May we come in?" Tone said in a soft, soothing voice .

"Yes, please have a seat." Mrs. Coker collapsed on the chair and looked up nervously.

"I'm sorry," Tone said softly.

Mrs. Coker looked at Tone and screamed no. Tone put his hand gently on her shoulder. "She called me the other day, said she wanted to come home and clean herself up before it was too late. She wanted to go back to school to become a nurse and needed my help. I was so happy she was coming over to talk. That was the last time I heard from her. She did that to me from time to time. Went days, even weeks, without hearing from her. I thought she did it again."

After talking about her addiction, she just didn't know who would want to hurt her Lizzy. She was a good person all in all. Tone put a hand on her and told her he was very sorry, and they would not rest until the person who did this would be caught. We followed a few leads on Elizabeth's and Lucia's cases, and at Midnight, we both went home.

At 9:00 a.m., we all pulled into the station like we followed each other. We went into the shop and started coffee. Gary and Lucy went to Curves. They got a list of women that may have worked out with Mary and Natasha. I called them yesterday and let them know Elizabeth and Lucia were not members. They split the list in half and went on their way. They spent all yesterday and half of last night and came up with nothing. We went over how each woman had been mutilated in the same exact way and lipstick was applied the same, and not one scene did we find any kind of evidence to point to any person. Gary and I said that we didn't think until now that the autopsy report was missing blood screening. "Now that you mention it," Lucy said, "neither did Natasha's." I smacked my head. With all that's going on, I didn't think about the lab. The local lab was undergoing construction to upgrade, and they had to send everything out. I called Peter and asked him if the blood work came back. He said he was just going to call, and he would be right over. We went over the lack of physical evidence. None of the women had any other wounds or bruises, except the mutilation. We were discussing how the killer got the women to lie still while he cut away at them when Peter walked in. He apologized that he didn't have the tox reports until now but went on to explain how each woman had a high level of aspirin, enough to render them unconscious, but not enough to kill them.

His opinion was that the killer had grounded up the aspirin and had it in a drink. As he or she was talking to the victims, they drank the aspirin, and once they were unconscious, then he started his work. Tone said we should go to the stores and ask if anyone purchased large amounts of aspirin recently. We all agreed that, like the knives, lipstick, and now the aspirin, nobody would really notice if anyone bought any one of these items. "Yeah, I think you are right," Tone agreed.

Another long day when Tone asked about Hot Shotz. I told him it's been three weeks since Lucia was found, and we had been working day and night, and I had not seen Nicole since then either, so I was going to her place that night. "Gary, Lucy while you are all here, I think after a few weeks of nonstop work, it might be a good idea to just take tomorrow off."

"Sounds good," they both said at the same time.

"Tone, how about you stop by for dinner tomorrow? We'll just hang out awhile." With a big grin, he asked what time. "How about 5:30?"

"I'll be there," he said.

On the way to Nichole's, I thought if they got along, it would be an easier home-work environment. It was late. We had drinks and moved into the bedroom. In the morning, I awoke early to fix breakfast. Nicole was already out of bed. *Not early enough*, I thought. I heard the shower. I went to the kitchen, made some eggs and pancakes, and brewed a fresh pot of coffee. A smile hit her face when she looked at the table. "I wanted to make you a nice breakfast. You beat me to it." We kissed and sat to eat. We talked about her days since I last saw her, then it turned to the cases. We talked and discussed different possibilities, and before I realized it, it was 2:30 p.m.

"I almost forgot to tell you I invited Tone to dinner at my place at 5:30." She looked a little upset but said that was fine. "Let's go shopping then." It was 5:30 p.m. sharp when we walked into the kitchen.

"Hi, Anthony," Nicole said as she gave him a friendly hug and kiss on the cheek.

"Hi, Nicole," in a flat voice, "I didn't know you would be here."

"I thought it would be nice for the three of us to hang out and get to know each other better," I said as I handed him a beer, "and besides, maybe Nicole could hook you up with one of her nurse friends."

"Yeah, sure," he said. I excused myself to go check on the grill. I thought about how Tone's attitude changed when he saw Nicole there. I thought it was weird, but Tone was somewhat weird and a loner type of guy. The steaks were done, and it's time to eat. When I went inside, it was as if nobody was there. I saw Nicole fixing the table.

"Where's Tone?"

"He went to get something from the car." The table and food were ready when Tone came in. He seemed a little better. As we ate, Nicole was asking Tone questions about him. Some he answered, some he didn't. He did not ask her one thing. She offered a little about herself.

He just looked at me and said, "That's nice." The evening ran on with small talk, and at 10:00 p.m., Tone excused himself and left. We discussed Tone for a while, how he was quiet and kept to himself too much. Nicole got a bad vibe from him and said she didn't know what it is, but something was not right with him. I told her he was just shy and didn't say much about himself. I told her, "I don't even know what he does on his off time." We went into the bedroom for another blissful night.

At 2:30 a.m., the phone rang. "Mecelli, yeah, where? I'll be right there." Nicole stirred under the blanket. I told her to go back to sleep and that I would call her later, and I was gone.

Great now, it's raining. It wasn't raining hard, just enough to get you soaked after a while. I was the last one there. I found John. He shook his head. I already knew there was nothing there. There never was. Why? I asked myself. I turned and walked toward the body. Gary, Lucy, and Tone were there. Lucy was holding the pocketbook this time.

"Hey, Peter."

"Hi, Joe."

"Anything?" I asked. Peter shook his head and zipped the bag. I stayed there in my own thoughts while everybody hurried to shut down the scene. I wondered why there was never any forensic evidence. *Could it be one of the CSIs*? I looked at each one of them doing their own thing. None of them looking even a slight bit nervous. *No, I knew them all for years, cannot be. How about Peter? No, Peter is too nice of a man, couldn't hurt a fly. Who? Why can't we put this together*?

"Are you staying all night?" Tone asked. I looked around. They were just finishing packing everything away. It was 6:30 a.m. I stopped at a diner on 209, bought four breakfast meals to go, and went to the shop. Tone had four coffees on the table. As I set each meal out, we ate. We discussed the events of the night. We cleared the table and got to work. As usual, nothing in the clothes. Lucy dumped the pocketbook. The usual woman things.

"Pull out the driver's license," I said. Maria Nancy Rosen, twenty-four years old, short brown hair, slightly overweight, shows she lived on Vista Maria Road, Cragsmoor. Just up the road from where the body was found.

"Lucy, go through the phone. Get some names, talk to them. Gary, go to JC Penney's and talk to people there. Tone and I will go to her house. Keep in touch as we all walk out." We drove up Gully Road, past the scene. A few people were milling around. A little boy answered the door. Must be nine or ten.

"Hi, is your mommy home?"

"No, my dad is. Dad!" the boy yelled. Dad came to the door.

"Mr. Rosen?"

"Yes."

"Does a Maria Rosen live here?"

"Yeah, my sister, is something wrong?" He started breathing heavily and shaking slightly.

"May we come in?"

"Who are you?"

"I'm Detective Anthony LaFonte, and this is Detective Joe Mecelli."

"Come on in."

Tone said, "Let's have a seat," in his low, soothing voice.

"He got her too?" he asked, tears starting.

"I'm sorry," Tone said with his hand lightly on his shoulder.

"She got home around nine last night and went out for a walk. I thought maybe her boyfriend picked her up. I tried to call her, but her phone is here on the counter."

"Did you call her boyfriend?"

"Yeah, but there was no answer."

"Do you mind if I look in her room?" I asked.

"Sure, upstairs, second on left." I went upstairs while Tone talked to the brother. I looked around. A few check stubs, a picture on the dresser, and not much more. She kept her room spotless. I went back down.

Tone stood up and told Randy we'd be in touch and, again, said softly, "I am truly sorry, and we will not rest until the person responsible is caught."

As we left, Tone said she was going to school to be an x-ray tech and working part-time at JC Penney. We went back to the shop to run a Joseph Crowler, the victim's boyfriend. No rap sheet. According to DMV, he held a class A license with an address of Burlingham Road, Walker Valley. As we pulled up to the Crowler residence, a Subaru pulled in, and a man with a UPS uniform got out. We pulled in behind him.

"Joseph Crowler?"

"Yes."

"I'm Detective Joe Mecelli, and this is Detective Anthony LaFonte. May we have a word with you?"

"Sure, come on in."

As we sat down, Tone said, "Do you know Maria Rosen?"

"Yeah, she's my girlfriend."

"When did you last see her?"

"Yesterday, why? Is she all right?"

"I'm sorry, we are homicide detectives.""

Oh my god," he kept saying. "Oh my god."

"Did anything unusual happen yesterday? Did you argue, fight?"

"No, we never argue. We were newly dating. We didn't even disagree on anything."

"How long have you been dating?"

"Four or five weeks."

"What time did you see her yesterday?"

"About 4:00. I have a Middletown area run; her shift was five to nine yesterday. I met her at Wendy's at four for dinner, then she went to work."

"You didn't talk to her after that?"

"Yeah, she called on her way home and said she had to study for a test today, so she was going home."

"What did you do last night?"

"I went over to the neighbor's house, had a few beers, played some cards."

"What time did you get home?"

"I don't know, 12:00–12:30."

"Then what?"

"Showered and went to bed. Why are you asking me this?"

"Just part of the investigation. Okay, we'll be in touch."

Tone put his hand on Mr. Crowler's shoulder in his soft voice. He said, "I'm truly sorry."

We went to talk to the neighbor. Yes, he was there playing cards 'til 12:00–12:30. They were positive he did not leave; they would have heard the car. We got in the car, and Gary called. They were back at the shop. They talked to about fifteen coworkers and nothing. I told him we were on our way. I told Tone on the way to the shop that he was doing a good job asking the right questions and doing good at breaking the news, but I was not hearing enough on his thoughts or what he thought. He looked at me and asked, "Isn't it frustrating not being able to solve these cases, wondering who could possibly be doing this? And why you can't catch this person? Does it make you feel powerless?"

Yeah, I thought to myself, *how can this person do this and not leave any trace*? I told him that these are cases that are tougher than you and there are cases you solve in minutes.

We walked into the shop. Gary and Lucy had their notes out, reading over each other's. Nobody said anything. They were lost in their own thoughts. I thought about each case. No defensive wounds, and the tox reports came back with high levels of cocaine. None of them had a coke habit. There was Elizabeth, but her drug of choice was meth, no report of coke, only in sales. I said out loud, "Do you think the killer could have a large amount of cocaine on a rag and grabbing them like that? You mean like instead of chloroform, they use coke? Yeah, it is probably easier to get coke."

I called Peter. He thought a moment, "I guess it could be, that would explain the cocaine in all the victims. Sure, it could be."

"Okay," I said, "that could explain how there are no defensive wounds. The victims are grabbed from behind with a cloth full of coke. They are startled and took a deep breath and ingest the coke. They may stumble a few times, and the killer helps them to his car, and soon they are so out of it, they don't know what's going on, and after, they are hacked up, they bleed out quickly."

Tone looked at me wide-eyed and said, "That's how it's done. It makes sense, I mean. Well, it's late. Let's pick it up tomorrow."

I went home too tired to shower. I just fell on the bed. I woke a few hours later, pulled my shorts on, and went on my run. I showered and called Nicole. A few minutes of small talk while I drank a glass of orange juice, and off to work I went.

I was the first one in and had to make the coffee. Peter came in. We chatted about drinks later. "I've been too busy, but yes, meet me at eight. You call John, I'll let the rest know." I decided to call for help from a profiler. He would be here this afternoon.

Tone came in looking tired. "What happened?" Thinking I could get something from his private life.

"Oh, just couldn't sleep," he said, and that was it. Gary and Lucy walked in, and I thought for a second about how they usually arrive at the same time, was something between them?

"Good morning," I said, "I called for a profiler. He will be here this afternoon."

"Good," they both said.

"I have never worked a case like this," Gary said. "I am getting frustrated not being able to find just the simplest little clue. This guy is good, and that's bad."

Lucy agreed, "It is almost unheard of to be doing all these murders and not leave one bit of evidence behind. There must be someone we are missing. Tone, can you get us the crime photos?"

"Sure, Everyone grab a seat and go over them." We all grabbed a seat, and we went through every photo. Just then, Jack Korso walked in.

"Detective Mecelli?"

I stood. "Hi, call me Joe. This is Gary, Lucy, Anthony. Everyone, this is Jack Korso, the profiler." After the handshakes, he looked at the board, the photos and names of the victims. He opened his book and started writing. He wrote every name in separate books, ages, hair color, height, and weight.

"Ready?" Jack asked. He wanted to see all the scenes.

"Gary and Lucy, could you go to Mrs. Rosen and see if Maria had any friends that called or came around and then check them out?"

"Sure, okay."

I grabbed the scene photos I had made for Jack. "Let's go!" I said.

We went to each scene crime scene. Each one had its own book. We spent about an hour at each scene writing and talking. We stopped at a local diner and ate. Jack hoped he could bring more light on the cases. I said we could use a spotlight if we had one. The cases were really trying our abilities. "I bet it is," Jack said. Jack told Tone these were cases that were not seen often, so don't get frustrated. These cases teach you more than you think. Tone just shook his head and asked Jack how long it will take him. Jack replied that hopefully, it be quick enough. We went back to the shop. I ask Jack if he had everything he needed. He said yes and said goodbye to everyone and was gone. We all plopped down in our chairs. "Well, let's do it again," I said.

Victim, Mary Spiel, twenty-seven years old, blonde, worked at Shoprite. Interviewed family and friends, nice woman, no kids, and we all read interview sheets, crime reports, looked at all the fifty short CSI reports, not much in the autopsy. High level of cocaine and speed, and cause of death: bled out due to mutilations. The only things left at the scene: victim's clothes neatly folded; victim's purse; knife wiped clean, commonly sold anywhere; and a tube of red lipstick, also wiped clean and sold in many stores. We made it through the third victim when we decided to call it a day. By going over every detail, we hadn't noted the time. It was 11:30 p.m. We were walking out when the call came.

"Mecelli."

"Yeah, where?"

"I am here with everyone. I'll tell them. We got another one." We got to the scene, we all pulled up in separate cars so we can go home and get some sleep after. There were two Ellenville units. They had taped off the area and were talking to three people. We walked toward the body. Office Janrel stayed with the callers, and Sergeant Story joined us. They noticed a dim light in the thicket, then a vehicle pulled away. They walked down here and spotted her. There she was, blood in the groin area, and a clown smile. The smile looked a little different, and clothes were not as neat. I sent Gary and Lucy to talk to the witnesses. Tone and I looked around. Footprint. I quickly shoved a stick in the ground so nobody would tramp on it. Just then, John and his crew showed up. I walked over to John with the excitement of a child on Christmas morning. "John, I got a footprint next to the body." The crew set up lights, and I went to it. I showed John the footprint. He put his measuring stick down and took a few pictures. He then mixed some plaster to make a mold. While the plaster was drying, we talked about how the killer might have been rushed. Then Peter walked up.

"Hey, guys."

"Hey, Peter," we both said.

"We have to find this guy or woman," Tone added quickly. John took the molded print away so Peter could get to work.

As he was looking at the body, he said, "Joe, the smile looks slightly different." He searched around the head, no lipstick. He noticed a slight bruise on the right side of her neck.

"Is that a bruise?" Tone asked.

He was acting strange, maybe he is exhausted, I thought. We all were.

"Yes," Peter said, "a very small one, but it is a bruise. I have to get her back to the morgue and get started." Without another word, she was in a bag and gone.

I told John we did not find the lipstick, but the knife was there. Gary and Lucy came back. They talked to every household on the street. Since it was a dead-end street, there were like ten houses. I told them to go home and get some sleep. We were almost through here, and we would meet at the shop around ten. We finished up at the scene. After four hours of sleep, I awoke. As I finished my run, I was feeling good. We all were in the shop a little before ten and started right away.

Gary and Lucy were going over their interviews. Two other people saw a car they didn't recognize. According to the witness by the scene, all they made out that it was a dark color SUV. The two people down the road said it was a dark green Chevy Trailblazer. Neither one looked at the plate or saw the driver. I told them about the footprint and the smile was a little different and the lipstick was not found. We were feeling good, the killer was starting to get sloppy. We dumped out the purse and searched for the wallet when her cell phone rang. Lucy answered, "This is Detective Lucy Pinia, whom am I talking to?" As I was listening to a one-sided conversation, I went through her wallet: Sally Freeman, a middle initial, 27 Park Street. Gary was holding a tube of lipstick with tweezers. Tone was getting an evidence bag. Just then, John came in and sat down. He looked like he was bursting with good news. Lucy finished up on the phone, and before she could say anything, John said they got a print on the knife, and the foot impression was clear. They ran the print and found no match, but at least they have a print. I told Gary and Lucy to go over the files on everyone listed on every victim and get the names to which one had fingerprints on file and compare them and give us a list of those who don't. The ones who didn't have prints on file, we would call them in and re-interview them and set down a clean can of soda, then take their prints off the can when they leave. They got the list together and gave it to John. He said he would make it a priority and hopefully have a list back in a couple of hours.

Lucy explained how the call was from Sally's husband, Hector. She didn't come home last night and didn't answer her phone. I sent her and Gary over to the morgue to see if Peter finished the autopsy. As Tone and I pulled into the drive on 27 Park Street, there were two teenage boys playing basketball at the end of the driveway. There was a garage with a hoop attached. We got out of the car, and the ball bounced toward us. Tone caught the ball. I thought he was going to start shooting with them but threw it back instead. Just then, a big Spanish man walked out.

"May I help you?" he asked.

Before I can open my mouth, I heard, "Yes, I am Detective Anthony LaFonte, and this is Detective Joe Mecelli. We are here about Sally Freeman." The boys looked at us wondering why we were here.

"Come on in," Hector said. Tone started asking questions right away. According to Hector, Sally left after the boys went to sleep at around 10:30 p.m. She was having a girl's night down at the local bar. He hadn't seen her or heard from her since. Tone asked him if they were arguing, if she was mad at him for some reason, or if he left the house last night. "No, why are you asking me this?" Tone explained that her body was found last night, and that we were homicide detectives investigating Sally's murder. I noticed he didn't have his usual soft, soothing voice. Tone asked him to come down to identify the body. Hector seemed upset, but not the crying and screaming. He said he would be down after he talked to the boys. Tone gave him a card and told him to call when he was coming

I thought about Tone's attitude on the way back to the shop. I figured he was tired and frustrated. I got a call from Gary. He suggested I go to the Coroner's office.

"Hi, Peter."

"Hi, hello, Joe."

"What do you have?" I asked.

"Where's Tone?"

"He's in the bathroom."

"Well," Peter said, "when I brought Sally in last night, I started the paperwork, and I felt really tired. So, I'm sorry I went home to sleep. I didn't want to miss anything due to lack of concentration. So today, I came in, and as I uncovered the body, the small bruise on her neck was larger now." I noted the bruising around her neck. Just then, Tone walked in.

"Hey, guys."

"Hi, Tone," we all said.

"Holy crap," Tone said, noticing the bruises on her neck. "What happened to her neck."

"Postmortem bruising," Peter said. "Sometimes, after the body sits, the bruises appear due to the blood shifting around because it is no longer flowing. So, I noticed the neck and started examining the body more closely. I noticed slight defensive wounds and found skin under one fingernail." He handed me a small ziplock plastic bag with a small sliver of skin.

We got him now, I said to myself. "How about the lipstick?" I asked, thinking it looked slightly different.

"I got a swab before I washed the body." He handed that over. "I also taped her hair." Taping her hair meant he put a large sheet of tape under her head and used a very fine comb. Anything that was loose in her hair fell onto the tape as to not lose any trace evidence. He handed me the tape and explained there were few light-colored short hairs and a few carpet fibers. Lastly, the mutilated area was a stabbing, not a cutting.

"Was the cause of death the same?"

"No, this one is death by strangulation."

We all left and went back to the shop. "It shouldn't be long now," Tone beamed.

"What?" I asked him.

"The killer got sloppy. He didn't have his usual time because he went to the wrong place. It wasn't as secluded as he thought, so he didn't have the time to fold the clothes properly and hack her the way he wanted."

"Well, that's one theory," I said.

I looked at Gary and Lucy. They were veteran detectives, and they looked like they were on the same page as I was. "What about the lipstick?" Gary asked Tone.

"There was something about it, and the tube was not left behind. In the killer's haste, he forgot to leave the tube."

"What about the print on the knife?" Lucy asked.

"Didn't have time to wipe it," Tone said.

"What about the strangulation?" I asked him.

"Maybe Sally is an addict and didn't respond the same, so he panicked and choked her to death."

"Yeah, maybe," Gary, Lucy, and I said in unison.

"Maybe we have a copycat," I said.

Tone's smile disappeared. "No, it has to be the same." Thinking he was getting frustrated and being new to homicide wanted to solve this one to get his life back.

"We'll see," I said.

Just then, John came in.

"Hey, John. I was just on my way to see you. I have some trace from Sally's autopsy for you."

"Trace?" he asked. It looked like he turned to our page.

"Yeah," Tone said, "we are finally gonna catch this son a bitch."

John looked at him. "Yeah, we'll catch all right, but will it be the same son a bitch? I have a list for you," John said. "I checked the other prints and nothing." I gave him the bags from Peter's office, and he gave me a list.

"Twenty-three people on the list," I said. Tone's phone rang. It was Hector. We had to meet him at the morgue in twenty minutes.

Hector pulled up, and I noticed his dark-green Chevy Trailblazer. "Nice car," I said as we walked inside.

"That's her," Hector cried as Peter pulled the sheet back to Sally's chin. Tone aided nothing.

"Mr. Freeman," I said, "could you come down to our office so we could get your statement and give you your wife's belongings?"

"Sure," he said, wiping a tear that formed on his eye. Down at the shop, I sat a freshly wiped can of soda in front of Hector. He looked at it and thanked me. Hector gave his statement, shifting around his seat. When he left, I put his can in an evidence bag and noticed there were already eleven cans in bags.

Gary and Lucy were busy, I thought. I put all the bags into a box and sent Tone over to John with them. "Tell him to check Mr. Freeman's first."

"You think he is the killer of his wife?"

"Yes."

As he left, Sergeant Story walked in. "Good evening, det."

"Hi, sergeant. What brings you here?" Noticing it was 8:30 already.

"Well, I'm here about the Freeman case. I checked the lumber yard at the beginning of Pine Street today and learned they have security cameras in the yard. I looked at the cameras, and they have on in the yard that faces the road. So, I looked it over. At 10:35 p.m., a dark-colored trailblazer goes up the road. At 10:50 p.m., a dark-colored trailblazer come back out. I brought a copy for you."

"Thank you, Sergeant Story."

"Call me Tom," he said.

"Well, thank you, Tom. Can I interest you in a cup of twelve-hour old coffee?"

"No thanks," Tom said, "I have to run, just wanted to bring this tape to you."

"Well, thank you, sergeant, I mean Tom."

Tone came back just as both Gary and Lucy were finishing up with two more people. I looked at them. They all looked exhausted. "Well, tomorrow's another day," I said.

I was a little late this morning. I met Nicole at the diner in Kerhonkson. Gary was in a room with a person from Lucia Lopez's case, and Lucy was in another room with another person from Natasha Brown's case. John walked in.

"We got a match," he said.

"Hector Freeman?" I asked.

"You got it," he said.

"Well, let's go, Tone. Thank you, John."

"No problem. Get me his swab for a comparison on the skin under Sally's nails."

"Will do," I said as Tone and I walked out. John stayed to let Gary and Lucy know about the print match.

We pulled into the driveway of Hector Freeman. The boys were there playing basketball with a few other kids. They stopped and watched us walk to the door. Hector came out, and we arrested him for the murder of his wife, and the boys screamed. We took him to the shop while the Ellenville officers waited for relatives to come for the boys. John was having the SUV flat-bedded to the lab. "You're making a mistake," Hector kept saying. We sat him in interview number two and left him there to sit. We watched him in the mirror for about ten minutes until the ADA (Assistant District Attorney) showed up.

Alex Fillmore was a round man, early sixties, and with pleasant attitude with a firm handshake. "Hi, Joe. How ya doing?"

"Fine, Alex. How's the Missus?"

"Good, Joe, good. Who do we have here?" Looking at Tone.

"Oh, Alex, this is Detective Anthony LaFonte." Tone flinched slightly at the handshake.

"Okay, Joe, fill me in quick, and we'll get started." We went over the first five victims quickly, then the sixth, Sally Freeman. We went over the evidence. Alex thought a minute. Thirty years in the prosecutor's office taught him to think and plan his interrogations quickly.

"Okay, let's go." He looked at me.

"I thought you could bring Tone in. Teach him a little."

With a shot loud laugh, he looked at Tone. "Time to go to class."

They went in. I stayed behind the mirror. "Hi, Mr. Freeman. I am Assistant District Attorney Alex Fillmore. I understand you were read and understand your rights, and you choose to speak to me."

"Yes. These detectives don't understand I am not guilty. I did not kill my wife."

"Okay, do you mind if I turn this on?" He pulled a tape recorder out of his briefcase.

"I don't mind. I have nothing to hide," he said. Alex put a fresh tape and turned it on.

"My name is Assistant District Attorney Alex Fillmore. I, along with Detective Antony LaFonte, are interviewing suspect Hector Freeman. Were you read your rights?"

"Yes."

"Do you understand your rights?"

"For now, yes."

"Okay, Mr. Freeman, could you tell me about the last time you saw your wife?"

"Well, the other night."

"What night was that?"

"Uh, Wednesday night."

"The eighteenth of August?" Alex asked.

"Guess so," Hector replied.

"Well, she was on the phone, and I heard her say 'see you around ten.'"

I asked, "Who was that?"

"She said it was her friend Marie. She and a few friends were getting together, and she was gonna join them."

"What time was the call?"

"I don't know, 9:30 I guess."

"Then what?"

"She went upstairs, showered, got ready, came into the living room kissed me, and said, 'If you're sleeping, I wake your ass up.'"

"What did that mean?" Alex asked.

"Well," Hector said softly, kind of in an embarrassed voice, "when she goes out, she kind of get, well you know."

"No, I don't know, she gets what?" Alex said with a grin.

In a very low voice, Hector said, "You know, horny."

"Did you say horny?" Alex asked in a loud voice.

Hector looked at him embarrassed. "Yes, that's what I said."

"So, you were not mad that she went out without you?"

"No, why would I? I knew what to expect when she got home."

"But she didn't come home, right?"

"No, she didn't."

"Did she come home and not want you this time?"

"No, she never came home," he yelled. "Why don't you guys believe me?"

"Did either detective tell you what they have to make them not believe you?"

"No," he said.

"Well, let me explain. They have the knife that you left at the scene.

"I didn't leave anything anywhere. I didn't do it, I tell you."

"Mr. Freeman," Alex said, "you didn't do a good job at wiping the knife, your fingerprint was found on it." Hector said nothing.

"We also have witnesses and a video camera that shows a dark-colored Trailblazer drive in and back out. What kind of car do you drive, Mr. Freeman?" He did not answer. Alex asked him again.

"I want a lawyer now," Hector screamed.

"Do you want to call one, or do you need a public defender?"

"I want to call one. Thank you."

I walked out to the shop. Alex came out. Tone brought Hector to the phone. He grabbed all the evidence we had. "Joe, I'm going back to the office. Will you bring me the results from John you have pending?"

"I will."

"Okay, book him in the county jail. Make sure his lawyer knows where or he can contact me."

"Sure thing, Alex."

"Oh, and Joe, good luck on the other cases. Hope you get the person soon."

"Thank you, Alex." And away he went. It was late when we booked Hector in the jail. I was meeting Peter and John at Hot

Shotz. Tone said he was tired and wanted to go home. He was going to stop in after he went home and changed. I told him I would not be there that long; we were taking the weekend off, and I was spending it with Nicole.

The ride was quiet. I dropped him off. "See ya Monday," Tone said.

"Yeah, okay." Then he slammed the door shut.

He must be really exhausted, I thought. I stopped at Hot Shotz. We talked about the copycat. John said he had the fiber and hair results. He was just waiting for DNA, but I could pick us what he had on Monday. "Great," I said, "at least we close one case, huh?" What kind of person can do this? First, mutilating these women like he does and not leave any kind of evidence whatsoever? Peter makes more of a statement than a question.

"Sometimes it may be bad to say, but sometimes, I'm glad I only deal with nonliving victims. I think I would be in the loony bin by now if I had to figure out and deal with the crazy profile that actually send them to me."

"I know what you mean, Peter," I said.

"Sometimes I think I should be in the loony bin with all the sick and twisted people I have dealt with in my career so far," John said, "it's not too late to change career paths and step over to CSI. I think you would be a fine field investigator."

"No, I think I'll pass. It may sound offensive, but I think I would be bored at CSI."

"Oh, thanks a lot, Joe, now I have a boring job. Maybe I'll be one of the craziest that you deal with someday. CSI snaps, goes postal out of boredom."

"You know what I mean, John."

"I know, just busting on ya."

"Yeah, I know," I said thinking how offensive I took that. "These cases are really weighing me down. I should have laughed and came back with something, and all I did was defend myself. I hope I don't take all this back to Nicole's."

I thought about the first case, *Did anyone stick out? Was there someone or something that we missed? No, we did a thorough job, oth-*

erwise, Gary and Lucy would have found something. I pulled into Nicole's driveway. I walked around for a few minutes. *Come on,* I said to myself, *think about Nicole and the lone overdue weekend with her.* Just then, she came outside.

"Joe, is everything okay? Are you all right?"

"Yes, everything is fine."

"I was afraid to come out."

"Why? You knew it was me, didn't you?"

"Yes, but you pulled up, and I watched you walking around out here. All I could think was you were trying to come up with a good excuse not to see me anymore." I could see tears in her eyes, and she was chewing her bottom lip.

I rushed over to her and held her tight. "No way, my darling. I would be the craziest man on earth to even think about leaving you." I felt her relax, a rush of breath, then a long, lingering kiss, that kind that makes you feel all funny inside.

She stepped back, wiped her eyes. "Well, what is the matter then?"

"I just wanted to get work out of my head before I came in. I don't want work to get in the way of you. I think it might help a little now I am away from you a lot. I don't want to be away from you when I am with you. You do know what I mean?"

"Yes," she said as she stepped in and held me tight. "Would it help if we went in, had a drink, and talked out it." I would never discuss my cases with any woman I have been with, and I guess that might be what pushed them away.

"Sure," I said, "I think it might help a little."

We went in, and Nicole poured us a drink. "I thought you caught the guy you were looking for?"

"No, that guy was a copycat. He found out his wife was cheating on him. He had a little information on the way the other women were killed. If he knew a little bit more and wasn't so sloppy, he might have gotten away with it."

"Anthony thinks he's the guy."

"How do you know?"

"Well, he stopped by just before you got here. Said he was kind of rude and wanted to apologize. I told him, 'You hadn't been here.' There is something about him, Joe. I don't know what, but I felt nervous talking to him."

I thought about how quiet he was and how he got out of the car. *Poor kid*, I thought. "We have been working long hours on these cases. He thought we had a major break and finally caught the guy, and then realized it," I said, "I think the frustration is getting to him."

"He will learn you to deal with it," she said.

She is right, I thought. I am starting to feel a little better. We talked a little about each case. How there was no one person that stuck out in each case. How, although the area is small, the victims ran in different circles, and there really wasn't one person that showed up in any other case other than the case we were working on. There were no drifters around that we could find.

"How about a couple of homeless guys that live around town?"

"No, it can't be them. First, they would need a vehicle. They can't dump bodies all over without one."

"Oh, yeah, duh," she said.

I laughed. "It was a good question," I said. I went on to tell her how we think the women were subdued by a mixture of cocaine and speed and how we think he does it.

"Oh, I never heard about that."

"We are keeping a few things quiet so we could tell like the last one, if it is a copycat or the real thing."

"Okay, now I get it," she said.

"If you leak everything out, then any man that wants to kill his wife or girlfriend could just blame it on the real killer. You got it dear?"

She finished her drink and said, "You look a little better." Before I could say anything, she stood.

As she opened her robe, she said, "Maybe this could make you feel even better." I picked her up and carried her to the bedroom. We were so into each other that we were the only ones on the planet. When it was unwittingly coming to an end, we were both drenched and out of breath. We both walked on wobbly legs to the shower. That's when we heard her phone.

She came back to the shower laughing. "What," I said.

"I am the on-call nurse today. They said they called three times. Did you hear anything?"

"No." I laughed. I was so high in the clouds with pleasure I didn't hear anything. She hurried out the door. I noticed then it was 9:30. We were talking all night, followed by the best lovemaking you can imagine. I hope she felt awake and alive as I did.

I went out to the car and got my running gear. I kept a pair of shorts and running shoes in the trunk.

Sometimes I go out for a run to clear my head. My head was clear, and I felt great, I thought. I got dressed and started my run. I thought about Nicole and how much I care about her. I thought about how good it felt to talk to her last night. I noticed I was in Ellenville. I ran farther than usual, I thought. Well, I feel better than usual. I circled around and started back. I thought about maybe buying a house somewhere and asking Nicole to move in. Then I heard a horn blowing and someone calling and waving me down.

"I was looking for you last night. I thought you might have gone to your cabin, so I got up early and drove up there. Where the hell were you?"

"Calm down," I said.

"I'm sorry, I just got worried."

"What are you looking for me for?"

"Well, I felt bad after you dropped me off last night. I just wanted to talk to you."

"Why didn't you call?"

"Well, I went by Hot Shotz, and you weren't there. Then I went to Nicole's. She said you didn't go there. Then I went to your place, nothing. So, I thought you might have gone to the cabin. I know there was no cell service there, so I got up early and drove up there and there was no sign that you were there. We must have missed each other at Nicole's. I drove by this morning. I didn't see your car."

"I know, I parked out back. Let me finish my run. I'll meet you at the diner in Kerhonkson in an hour, okay?"

"Okay," he said and got in the car.

As I finished my run, I thought about how weird he was acting. He was always a little weird, maybe I just never realized it. I thought it was just rookie nerves. His first case turned into cases, and he was trying to find a way to deal, I thought as I was getting dressed. I looked at my phone, no missed calls. *Oh, how sweet*, I thought.

I pulled up to the diner. Tone was already there. I went in and sat down.

"How long you been here?"

"I came right here."

"You've been here an hour?"

"Yeah."

"Tone, do you have anything to do when you're not working?"

"No, I usually either study or go for a drive."

"Tone," I said, "you need to find someone to spend your time with. When was the last time you been with a woman?"

"A woman?"

"I know you like women, right?"

"Of course, I'm not gay," he said angrily.

"I didn't say you were. It's just you never talk about anything outside of work. You are going to be a great detective, but I found that you need to find someone you care about and can talk to. You will be surprised on how good you will feel." I thought about how I felt when I got to Nicole's last night. We talked for hours. I felt great on one hand, if I would have known these years ago, I probably would not have had so many failed relationships. On the other hand, I probably would not have met Nicole in this way. *Oh well, better late than never*, I thought.

"What do you mean talk, talk about what?"

"We, whatever you need to talk about." I thought a moment, then the waitress finally came. "Can I have a coffee and a ham and cheese omelet?" She looked at Tone.

"Just more coffee," he said.

I said, "Tone, how do you feel about not being able to catch this person?"

"Bad," he said. I waited for him to say more, but that was it.

"Why do you feel bad?" I asked.

"Because," he said. I can see he was thinking about what to say, so I waited. The waitress brought my coffee and filled Tone's cup. I smiled, she smiled back. "Because I am," Tone said, "I mean, I study a lot about crime scenes and forensics, and I can't do this," and then he stopped.

"Do what?" I asked. "Homicide? You want to go back to patrol?"

"No," he said, "patrol is not where I'm going anymore."

"So what? What can't you do?"

"I just think that you have been in homicide for a long time. You are a smart guy and should be able to figure this out. Maybe I am getting in the way, that's why you can't solve this."

"You can't think like that, you are pretty damn smart yourself, and by bringing in Gary and Lucy, they can't even figure this out, so don't think that you are the reason this case isn't solved by now."

"Maybe you're right."

"Okay, now let's forget about work. What do you have planned for the rest of the weekend?"

"Nothing," he said.

"Well, I think you should go out tonight, you're a handsome young man. You shouldn't be just studying or driving around, you should be going out, enjoying the company of some hot young ladies."

"Yeah, maybe you're right. Maybe I'll go to New Paltz later and find me some nice college girls."

"There you go, now you're thinking. Feel a little better?"

"Yeah, I guess so."

"Good, now order something to eat. You're going to need your strength later."

We ate, talked about how nice the day was, how Tone was going to find two or three lovely young ladies tonight, and won't be able to walk for a week. "What are you going to do?" Tone asked.

"I thought I would go shopping and bring Nicole up to the cabin." Oh, the thought brought a smile to my face. The cabin was deep in the woods. You could only drive halfway in. I had a shed at the end of the road with two four-wheelers. You would need to take the four-wheelers the rest of the way to the cabin. The cabin was built by a small lake. My uncle built it years ago and left it to me when he died. I had plenty of cell service, but I tell everyone I don't, so I'm not bothered when I'm there. The thought of Nicole and I swimming naked made me stir. I had to come back to the table now, or I would be embarrassed when I stood. Tone stood without a smile. He said, "Have fun, I'll see you Monday."

"Yes, knock 'em dead tonight," I said. As I paid the check, I saw Tone looking at me funny.

"What do you mean by that?" he asked.

"Just have a good time, I mean."

"Yeah, you too," he said as he walked out.

We were walking to our cars when he asked me if we should be taking a weekend off. I looked at him. "Why shouldn't we," I asked him.

"Well, we have five open cases and one pending. Don't we have to make sure everything is ready for trial in the Freeman case?"

"I'm sure it will be fine. Alex has everything that we had, John has the hair and fiber reports. I am sure the DNA will be in soon. Everything in the Freeman case is fine."

"Well, what about the others?"

I thought for a moment. I told him if he needed to talk to someone I can't just leave now. "Come on get in," I said walking toward my car. "You can help me shop." With a big grim, he got in the car.

"Why do you think we can't catch this guy?" he asked.

"I don't know," I said. "Whoever it is, he or she is very smart and very careful." I must have been going a little too fast. The lights I saw behind me came closer. I pulled to the side and watched the trooper walked to the car. He leaned in.

"Oh, Tony," he said.

"Hi, Tom, what's up?"

"You guys were doing sixty back there. You know it's only forty-five, right?" I pulled out my shield.

"Oh, you're Tony's partner?"

"Yes, I am. Joe Mecelli," I said extending my hand.

"Tom Bruni," he said.

"You guys working?"

"No, we are going shopping. Well, we are discussing the cases, so maybe we are working."

"Well, I didn't recognize the car."

"Yeah, I'm sorry," I said. "I'll slow it down a bit."

"All right," he said.

"Hey, Tony, what are you doing tonight? I haven't seen you in a while. Want to do something tonight?"

Tone looked at me, I shook my head. "Sure," Tone said.

"I was thinking about going to New Paltz or Poughkeepsie. Want to go?"

"Sure, I get off around 4:30. I'll give you a call when I get home."

"Okay, good," Tone said.

"I would like to stay and talk, but I really have to go."

"Yeah, okay, you guys take it slow," he said.

"I will, Tom, and it was nice meeting you."

"Yeah, you too, Joe. I'll call you later, Tony."

"Okay, Tom, don't work too hard."

As we pulled away, Tone said he used to work with Tom. They went out after work a few times and lost touch pretty much when he went to homicide. "Well, it would do you some good hooking up tonight. But you better bring separate cars."

"Why?" Tone asked.

"Well, what if you and Tom hook up with hotties?" We got back to Tom's. He had a three-bedroom house over in Rosendale. "He doesn't have a steady? I'm sure he would have said something."

"Yeah, I guess you're right. But anyway, he said what about the case. Some nights I lose sleep over it."

"I'm sure we'll get him soon."

"Yeah, but we got nothing to on," he said.

"The son of a bitch doesn't leave us anything to work with."

"I'm sure he will slip up and leave some kind of clue."

"Yeah, but when? How many women will he kill?"

That's something I didn't want to think about, I thought. "I don't know," I said. "The local police, state and sheriff have extra cars around. Maybe the person will get spooked and stop."

"You think if he stops, we have enough time to catch him?" Tone asked.

"I hope so," I said. "Now what kind of steaks you think I should get?" Trying to change the subject.

"New York strips are good."

"Yeah, I think you're right." We finished up shopping. We talked about catching this person and taking a whole week off. Maybe we will go to Tone's cousin's place in Florida, do some deep-sea fishing. "Okay," I said. "I got plenty of food and drinks. Got some wine and beer. I think I need to stop and get some fuel for the generator. The quads have enough gas, so I have everything," I said. I pulled up next to his car. "You feel a little better after talking?"

"Yeah, a little," he said.

"Okay, I'll be back tomorrow night, and I want to hear all about your night, so you better have a good time."

"Yeah, I will. I'll call you tomorrow, all right?"

"Have fun," I said.

"Yeah, you too," he said as he shut the door.

As I drove home, I thought about what Tone asked. You think if he stops, we have enough to catch him? Why did he have to ask that? It's something that I thought about, but just pushed the thought away. In my eleven years, I never had a case unsolved. I packed some clothes and headed to Nicole's.

She was wearing a skimpy white top and short blue shorts. Everything I was thinking disappeared. I got out of the car. "Excuse me, ma'am, I have a report that some woman washing her car is carrying a concealed weapon."

"Well, officer, unless you think this sponge is a weapon, I think you have the wrong address."

"This is the address I was given, ma'am."

"Well, as you can see, there are not many places in this outfit I can hide anything If you would like to step into the house, you're more than welcome to search me."

"I think that would be a good idea, just so I know I did a thorough investigation, that is."

"Okay, can I rinse the car first?"

"Sure, but I'll be watching closely."

"I'm sure you will." She smiled as she rinsed the car, and water was getting all over her as well as the car. Her white top, now see-through, and she bent over to rinse the wheel wells. Her ass was swaying slightly as to tease me. When the car was rinsed, she turned to me, pushing her chest out slightly. Her top was totally soaked, sticking to her like a second skin totally see-through. Thought of the wet T-shirt competition, I said, "You're that winner."

"Of what?" She smiled. "Ready to go in?"

"Oh, yes, I mean after you, ma'am." As I followed her, I couldn't help but stare at her backside. Her shorts looked like they were painted on. I tripped on the first step.

"Are you okay?" she asked with a smile.

"Yes, I am, ma'am. I think it's time for a strip search," I said as I peeled off her top.

As we finished, her phone rang. She took the phone to the other room. I could hear her talking angrily but couldn't make out what she was saying.

"Everything okay?" I asked.

"Yeah, that was my brother. He wants money again."

"I didn't know you had a brother," I said.

"Yeah, I don't talk much about him. He drinks day and night. I tried many times to put him through rehab, but he never stays long enough. I pretty much gave up on him."

"Is he married?"

"No, he was. She left him about fourteen years ago."

"So," she said changing the subject, "you gonna help me get some things together?"

"Yeah," I said going to her dresser. "This is all you need," I said as I pulled out a long shirt."

She laughed. "I don't get to bring no clothes?"

"Nope," I said. "There's nobody around. We can spend the whole time in the buff."

"Okay," she said, throwing a few things in a bag. We made sure everything was turned off and locked up and got in the car.

"Do we need to shop?"

"Nope. I have everything in the truck already."

"Okay, let's go then."

As we drove, I asked her about her day. She had to go in because a patient had surgery, and she had to do post-op stuff. I told her how I met Tone on my run, and we went to the diner, then shopping, and about our conversation.

"I get a bad vibe from him," she said. "I don't know what it is, but I don't think it's normal for a twenty-three-year-old to be so secretive. You really don't know much about him, do you?"

I thought for a minute. "I really don't know much. I've never been to his apartment. He doesn't really talk about his private life. He just likes his privacy," I said. "Although I admit it's weird, but I wouldn't say it's not normal. I think maybe he had a bad life so far and had an issue with getting close to people. I think he needs to talk to someone."

"Well, you're his partner. Don't you guys talk about things?"

"Yeah, sometimes we do. He talks a little more than he used to. Well, this is as far as we go by car," I said as we pulled next to the storage building.

"What do we have to walk the rest of the way?"

"Yeah," I laughed, "all the way to the door."

I unlocked the chain and pulled the door open. There were two four-wheelers and a small trailer inside. "What happens if someone breaks in?"

"Well, if you notice, there is a solar panel on the roof, and if you look at the four-wheelers, there are thick steel plates around the axles. This nail right here is a switch." I pushed the nail upward, and the plates swung from around the axles. I started them up, hooked the trailer up, and pulled them out. I locked the building up and unloaded the care car into the trailer. I kissed her and hopped on the quad with the trailer. "Last one up is a rotten egg."

"I guess I'm a rotten egg then," she said as she got on the quad. The trail was a little overgrown, but we made it up just fine. It was getting dark as we finished bringing stuff in.

"I'll start the generator," I said, grabbing the two cans. We have the generator hooked up to a fuel tank. I poured in the fuel. It was half full, I noticed as I started it.

I went in and gave her the grand tour. It was a two-bedroom A-frame. We hooked a pump down in the small lake. The water was cleaner than any bottled water. Years ago, we dug a small septic system so we can have the convenience of home.

"This place is beautiful," she said, looking around. "That is the nicest fireplace I have ever seen."

"Thank you. I put it in myself." Remembering how long it took me to gather enough stone to make it. "I don't know about you, but I'm starving," I said. "I'll go get the fire going." Out back, I put in a big patio with all the field store I found, then put in a nice barbeque pit in. I stacked in some wood and got a nice fire going. Nicole brought out the two steaks and two potatoes wrapped in foil.

"Oh my God," she said, "this place is like a dream," as she looked around. I edged the patio with stone walls with a fieldstone cap. I put the steaks and potatoes on and stood next to her. By now, the moon was up, showing on the lake. "It is beautiful," she said. "I can't wait to see it in the day." As the steaks and potatoes were done, I threw on some vegetables. We ate by candlelight. "I can get used to this," she said.

"I think this is where I'm retiring to," I said.

"How about me?" she asked.

"That would be nice," I said. We cleaned up, and I started a fire.

We sat in front of the fire. She excused herself and went up to the bedroom. I didn't notice her come back down. When she walked in front of me, she said, "Well, I'm dressed." Her naked body glistened in the light from the fireplace. "Are you gonna get dressed?" she asked.

"Right away." I stood and ripped my clothes off. We made love listening to the wildlife outside. We both fell asleep in each other's arms in front of the fireplace. We awoke to the sun stretching across the room as it was rising. We both showered, and I made breakfast.

"I can't wait to get out and look around," she said as she walked toward the door.

"You gonna put some clothes on?" I asked watching her walk with only slippers on.

"No, you said I don't need any on, do I?"

"No, you don't," I said following her out with not even slippers on.

The backyard was cleared and seeded to make for a nice lawn, down to a small beach that took me two full summers to haul up enough sand for next to the beach. Next to the beach was a small dock with two Jet Skis.

"It must have taken a long time to get it like this."

Yeah, I thought. It certainly was hard work, but well worth it. "Just a little," I said. She ran down to the beach and dove into the water. I watched as she walked out. *Well, worth it*, I said to myself as she walked up to me.

"Well, what do you have planned for me?" she asked standing in front of me, I took it all in; her hair, back, water dripped down her erect nipples, and hands on those hips. I heard her say, "I see what you have in mind," as she looked down. We made love in the sand. "Are you sure your forty-one?" she asked. "You make me feel like a teen again," as we ran toward the water. We swam and laid on the beach for hours.

"Stay here, I'll be right back," I said. I went to the house, threw some sandwiches together, grabbed a bottle of wine and two glasses, and went back to the beach.

"You're gonna spoil me," she said.

"I don't want to go back." As we ate, we talked about the cases a little. She asked if I thought someone on the force might be involved since nothing is ever found on the scene. "It's funny you say that. It has crossed my mind, but I just can't think of any. No one looks or acts differently."

"I have a bad feeling about Anthony." I felt anger building when she said his name.

No, he may be a little different, but that does not mean he is a serial killer. I took a few deep breaths. *She is just trying to help*, I thought. I took a sip of wine. "Besides, he is working really hard on these cases. He would be trying to throw me off, and he isn't."

Sensing my anger, she said, "How about we check out the Jet Skis?"

"Let's go," I said finishing my wine. "I'll race ya." She ran toward the dock, and I watched her.

When she got there, she turned around. "Come on, what are you waiting for?"

"I have to get the keys, they are in the house." As I went toward the house, I thought about asking her to move in with me. I think I'm falling in love with her. I love being around her, although these cases keep me away too much. I'm sure we would solve them soon. She got me to open up and talk about things I never had before. Yes, I would ask her on the drive home. I grabbed the keys and the ball with the handle. I ran down to the dock.

"What's this ball for?" she asked while I got the machines running.

"It is used for water tag," I said. I threw the ball into the water and jumped on my machine. "You ever ride one these?"

"Yeah, a few times," she said.

"Okay, let's ride around a bit, then I'll grab the ball. I'll be the it first." We rode around awhile. When I saw she can ride pretty good, I grabbed the ball. She was good. It took me about six or seven throws to get her. We played for a while and parked the machines. "I think we better started cooking. It's getting late." As I made dinner, she packed up our stuff. We cleaned up and put everything away.

She walked over and grabbed me from behind. "How about one for the road?" she asked. I didn't have to say anything. It was amazing, a perfect end to a perfect weekend. We got dressed and loaded our things in the trailer. I followed her down the path. I thought about the words I would use. I had figured out by the time we reached the garage. We unloaded the trailer and got the machines locked up. It was almost dark by the time we got in the car and headed home.

"Joe, I want to thank you for this weekend, it was absolutely beautiful. I loved it.""

You're very welcome," I said thinking this was the perfect time.

"Nicole, I was thinking. We have been getting along very well." She smiled and held my hand. "I know it has been a long time, but

I feel comfortable and safe with you. You showed me I can open up and talk about anything with you. I was hoping we can step up our relationship and move in together." Her hand loosened in mine, and she was quiet for a while. "Is it too quick?" I asked.

"I don't know, Joe. I have never got that far in a relationship."

"You have never lived with anyone?"

"No, not yet." I looked at her. "It's just that I was eight years younger than my brother. He was thirty and, on his way up, already a junior supervisor in a big bank in the city when his wife left. He went on a downhill spiral and still today has not recovered."

"Why did his wife leave?"

"They had a son early on, and only one of them was able to advance. He worked long hours while taking night classes at the college. So, she said she was stuck home taking care of the baby alone and can't do it no more. That's what was in the note."

"She left him with the baby?"

"Yeah, well, he was seven by then. She just left and never came back. That was hard for me to see, and I stopped going over there. So for about fifteen or sixteen years, I have not seen or heard from him until about six months ago. He called me looking for money. I send him some when I can."

"How about your nephew?"

"Well, it's probably stupid, but I kind of blamed him, and I never saw him again." I didn't know what to think, so I sat quietly. "Please, just give me a little time, Joe. I really like you," she said, squeezing my hand.

I smiled. "Sure," I said, "I will wait forever for you." She unbuckled her belt and slid over next to me. We drove a while in silence.

"Joe, if you want to stay over, we should stop in the store."

"I would love to," I said. "I just have to go to my place and grab some clothes." We went to my place. "I might as well bring my stuff in since I'm here."

"I'll help," she said. We brought my stuff in and put it away. While I was grabbing my stuff, she said I had a few messages. I listened to them. John, Peter, and Tone wondering if I was back, and they would see me tomorrow.

"Seems like good friends you have Joe."

"Yeah, they are like family." We stopped at the store on the way to Nicole's. "What do we need?" I asked.

"I think we need milk, eggs, and whatever you want to go with eggs."

"How about ham," I answered grabbing some ham steaks.

"That's fine," she said. "I'll grab some English Muffins," she added. By the time we got to her place and put everything away, we were both exhausted and fell right asleep. As I walked in from my run, I could smell a wonderful combination of coffee, ham, and eggs.

"Smells good," I said. "I'll be right out." I hurried into the shower and went out in a robe. Everything was on the table. She smiled as I walked into the kitchen.

"Hungry?" she asked.

"Starving," I said. We both sat to eat. "I just want you to know that it's not that I don't want to live with you, Joe. I just need a little more time."

"I know," I said. "I understand. When you're ready, I'll be here."

"Thank you, Joe." We made small talk as we ate. It's not that I wanted to leave, but I was getting kind of anxious to get back to work. I was hoping this couple of days off would clear everyone's mind, and someone should stumble across something.

As I pulled up to the shop, I noticed Tone's car was there. When I went in, Tone was looking at case files.

"Hey, Tone."

"Oh, hi, Joe. I was just reading through, see if I can find something."

"Anyone else here yet?" I asked.

"No, just me."

"Well, how did your weekend go? Did you go out?" I asked.

"Yeah, I went out."

As I walked over to make coffee wondering why he didn't start it, he just sat there. I got the coffee going and said, "Yeah I went out, is that all I get?"

"Well, how did your weekend go?" he asked. I told him about the nice dinner and how we talked and how we discussed maybe someone in law enforcement might be the killer, leaving out the part where she mentioned his name.

"Do you really think that, Joe?"

"Well, the thought entered my mind a few times, but I don't think so." Just then, Gary and Lucy came in.

"Good," Gary said. "Someone made the coffee. I was running late and didn't stop."

"Good morning," Lucy said. "How was everyone's weekend?"

"Good," Tone said. "Joe was just saying he thinks the killer maybe someone in law enforcement." Everyone was quiet. Gary made his coffee and sat down.

As I looked at each of them, I could tell they were deep in thought. Lucy started first. "Let's just say we look at it that way. Where do we start?"

"Well," Gary said, "I think we could probably rule out the ordinary patrolmen, unless of course, they have a lot of knowledge about forensics."

"Why would they have to know about forensics?" Tone asked.

"Well, if you look at each scene," Lucy jumped in, "there are no tire tracks. There are no footprints, no fingerprints, no fibers, and no DNA."

"Maybe he is just careful not to leave anything behind, and also," Tone added, "if anyone saw a patrol car in the area, nobody would go over to see what he was doing, so he would have plenty of time to do what he wants." But nobody reported they had seen any vehicle stopped at any location. Tone thought for a moment. "Yeah, but he could have parked his car and walked a short distance. The victims could have still walked. They were drugged before they were killed."

"That's true," Gary said. "Then it could have been anyone who walked them there then."

"Anyone can be very careful not to leave anything behind," I said.

"I think we could say something may have been left," John said. We all were into our conversation that we didn't notice him come in.

"What do you mean?" I asked.

"Well, there was a small amount of powder found in the blood. We figured it was probably from the victims. Maybe putting baby powder after a shower, but it could be from an ordinary latex glove."

"Why didn't you tell us before?" I asked.

"Well, we can't tell for sure that it comes from gloves, or the women put it on themselves."

"Was it found on all of the women?" Gary asked.

"No," John said, "only three of them."

"Latex gloves," Tone said. "That could explain why there are no prints."

"Is there anything else we don't know, John?" I asked, and John said no.

"Well, did everyone have a nice weekend?" John asked. Everyone smiled thinking about what they did.

"Yeah," everyone said, "how about you?"

"Painted my garage, so no, not really. Anyway," John said, "I have the rest of the Freeman evidence."

"Okay, good," I said. "Now which three women did you find the powder on?"

"I will have to check and get back to you."

"Good, want some coffee?"

"Sure, why not." We started our discussion back up. John said if this powder came from a latex glove, then it could be someone in the medical field, or it could be anyone because you could buy latex gloves from any supermarket. As we were talking, Jock Korso, our profiler, came in. "Hi, Jack, you done already?"

"Yeah, so is everyone. I made this a priority. Maybe we can stop this guy or woman before someone else gets killed."

"What do you mean guy or woman?" I asked.

He placed a folder in front of me and walked over to the coffee pot. "I believe it is a woman," he said.

"A woman?" I asked.

"Why are you surprised he thinks it's a woman?" Tone asked.

"Well, most serial killers are male," Lucy said, "hardly ever a woman."

"Well, then why do you think it's a woman?" Tone asked Jack.

"Well, a couple of things. The fact that all the women are drugged."

"Well, a man can drug a woman," Tone said.

"Yes, that's true," Jack said. "However, a woman may not have enough strength to carry another woman from the car, but she can help a staggering woman to walk, so she drugs them. Second, the clothes are removed and folded neatly in a pile, starting with the largest piece to the smallest. The lipstick used was a very common brand and the exact shade. Most men would just get a certain color, not paying too much attention to the brand or shade. If you ever look in a makeup section, you will notice many different brands, and there are many different shades of each color."

"So, you don't think a man would take the time to pick the exact color and shade of lipstick?" Tone asked.

"Yes, it is possible that he could, but it would take a certain type of man to do that."

"Do you have a certain type of man in mind?" Tone asked.

"Well, I believe if it is a man, he would be very meticulous about everything in his life. A very neat and clean person where everything in his life would be in order and probably routine. So, we could possibly be looking for a Felix Unger type of man."

"Who is Felix Unger?" Tone asked.

"Years ago, there was a TV show call *The Odd Couple*," Gary explained. "It was about two men sharing an apartment. Oscar was, well, he was a slob, left everything all over the place. While Felix, he was always cleaning and straightening up the place. Everything had to be neat and clean"—I laughed—"Oscar used to stomp his dirty feet and move things around just to bet Felix going. It was a funny show."

"Yeah, I'll bet," Tone said.

"What's wrong with having a neat place?" he added.

"Nothing," Lucy said, "but Felix went a little overboard."

"So, we are looking for a Felix Unger?" Tone asked.

"Anything else, Jack?"

"I believe she is from the area. She knows pretty much all the back roads and where to leave the bodies where they will be found relatively fast yet have enough time to do her thing."

"What do you think about what she does to these women?" Lucy asked.

"Well, I believe something in her life upset her mentally, and it may be her way of getting revenge."

"So, you think she—" I was interrupted by Tone.

"Or he."

"Okay," I said, "she or he is doing this to get back at someone?"

"I believe she is," Jack said looking at Tone. He opened his mouth as if to say something but thought better of it and said nothing. Jack finished his coffee, threw his cup in the garbage, and looked at his watch. "Crap," he said, "it's four o'clock already? I have to go."

"We discussed all the major stuff, you have the report. You want to order dinner?" I asked Jack.

"No, I have to be somewhere at five. If I don't leave now, I'll be late. It was nice seeing you guys again. Anthony, nice to meet you," and he was gone.

"What are you guys going to order?" John asked.

"I don't know," I said.

"I was thinking Chinese?"

Everyone thought a moment and said, "Yes, that's good."

"All right," John said pulling out ten dollars, "order me subgum wonton and an order of wings. I'll run back to the office and get the reports on the powder on the three women, and I'll be back." When John left, we got our orders together and called it in.

"They will deliver," they said.

We took the downtime to talk about our weekends. I told them about mine, how we went up to the cabin, swam, and went jet skiing, leaving out a few details. Gary didn't really do anything; he cut the grass, drank some beers, and took a ride on his motorcycle. His wife didn't like to ride. Lucy cleaned up the house, went swimming with the kids, and went to the movies. Tone didn't say much; he scrubbed down his apartment, washed, and waxed his car. I asked him how his night out went. "All right" was all he said.

Gary asked, "You scrubbed down your apartment? What does that mean?"

"Well, I sweep the ceiling and walls so no cobwebs form, then I wipe down the walls and cabinets, vacuum the furniture, steam clean the carpets, dust and mop," Tone said proudly.

"Sounds like we should call you Felix," Gary said laughing.

"What's wrong with having a clean place?" Tone asked.

"Nothing," I said, "he's just teasing you, that's all."

"Yeah," Gary said, "just joking." Just then, the food came. I paid him, gave him a tip. As he was leaving, John came in.

"Just in time," he said. He set his folder on the side as we set the food out. We made small talk as we ate. When we finished, Tone said he will clean up. Gary, Lucy, and John went out for a smoke.

"Is anything wrong?" I asked Tone.

"No, why?" he asked.

"It seemed like you were getting upset when Gary was messing around with you."

"It's just I thought he was trying to say something. We just finished talking about what type of man the killer could be, and I mistook him," Tone said, almost nervously.

"I thought he was just joking," I said. "It's good that you are serious about your job, but you can't let your job take a hold of you." The others came in, the table was cleared and wiped down.

We gathered some files; John got his folder, and we went back to work. "Okay, John," I said, "what women had powder?"

"Let's see," he said opening his folder, "Mary Spiel, Natasha Brown, and Maria Rosen." We got their files out and added it in. Tone added it to the board. We have a big board where all the women's pictures and names with where they worked, lived, age, height, hair color, built, and eye color. Now on these three women, we needed to reinterview the people that were closest to them to see if we could find out if they used baby powder.

"Let's start with Mary Spiel." We went through her file. "We can talk to her parents, sister, and close friends."

"Okay, now Natasha? Let's see, she had an ex-husband, a sister, and parents."

"How about Maria? Parents and two close friends."

"Okay, now we have some names. First thing tomorrow, we can start interviewing." We talked a little more and decided to call it a day. Everyone left except Tone.

"I'm glad you stayed. I want to see how your night went."

"Well, we went over to New Paltz. There were not many people cause it's summer, but we made do. There were a few nice girls there. It was slow going at first, but as the night went on, it got better. I started talking with a very nice-looking woman with long black hair and brown eyes."

"How old is she?" I asked.

"She is twenty-two, from Kingston."

"Does she go to the college?"

"Yeah, she is studying to be a lawyer. She is very smart and outgoing."

"Did she go back to your place?" I asked.

"No, I didn't ask her."

"Why not?" I asked.

"I don't know," he said.

"Tone, I'm your partner, and I am trying to be your friend. You need to open yourself up a little bit. You're like a closed door," I said. "You need to know if I can help you I will, you can trust me."

"I know," he said, "it's kind of hard. I really didn't have anyone I could turn to when I was growing up. I just learned to keep it to myself."

"Well, I've known you for almost a year now," I said. "Anyway, I know where you live, but I have never been inside. I have never been inside. I don't really know what you like to do or even too much about you. If we are going to be partners, we should know a lot more about each other than we do."

"Yeah, you're right," he said.

"Now tell me, what's her name?"

"Leah, her name is Leah," Tone said. "She wants to be a teacher."

"You gonna see her again?"

"Yeah, I think so."

"You got her number?"

"Yeah."

"Good, go home and call her. I'll see you in the morning."

"I think I will. Goodnight, Joe," he said as he walked out.

"Goodnight, Tone." I gathered my stuff and went to Nicole's.

I told her I was going home tonight, so when I got to her place, she was asleep. When I went to the bedroom, she woke up. "I thought you were going home," she said as she got out of bed."

"I was going to, but I changed my mind."

"How was your day?" she asked. "Would you like a drink?" We were sitting in the living room talking about the day. I told her how Tone's night went, how he met a nice young woman and how he wanted to wait until after we get the killer to start a relationship.

"Why?" Nicole asked.

"Why what?" I said.

"Why wait until after the case is done?"

"I don't know. Maybe he wants to be focused on his first case."

"I don't know about him," she said.

"Why do you keep saying that? What do you think is wrong with Tone?"

"I don't know. There is something wrong when a young, attractive man doesn't have girls all around him. Do you think he might be gay?" she asked.

"Why would you say that?"

"Well, look at him. He is a very neat person. His clothes are a little too neat and always match a little too much for a single, young man. You never see him or his car even a little dirty or rumpled. I can only imagine what his apartment looks like, probably a little too neat for any woman, and he only says what he has to. He's a keep-to-himself type of person, it's almost weird."

"He is just a clean, neat type of guy with some childhood problems. It doesn't make him weird," I said.

"I don't know," she said. "There is just something about him I can't figure out just now." I couldn't help thinking that she is right. There is something about him. Every time his name comes up, she always tells me the same thing. There is something, but what? Maybe I will have to figure out what."

"Do you want to, Joe?"

"Huh, want to what?" I was lost in my own thoughts; I didn't notice Nicole stood up and wanted to go to bed.

"Do you want to come to bed?" she asked again.

"You bet," I said.

"Not for that," she said. "I'll take care of you, but I am too tired," she added.

"Okay, I'll settle," I said following her to the room. It didn't take long, and I was good, and she rolled over and was asleep.

My mind went back to the lake. We could not find any connection between the women. I thought about that for a while. *There just wasn't any connection, nothing in common; didn't run in the same circle, didn't know the same people. There was no evidence left behind: no tire tracks, footprints, and fingerprints. There were no fibers, no DNA, nothing. Okay, there was some powder. Could the powder be from latex gloves, or maybe the women used powder after their showers? All the scenes, the clothes were folded neatly, and the murder weapon was left behind. I was thinking it could be someone who knows about forensics. Tone knows about forensics. Could it be him? He does kind of fit the profile. He doesn't want to start a relationship until after the killer was caught. Could it be him? No, it couldn't be him. He is determined to catch this person. It just couldn't be him,* I thought as sleep took hold of me. I woke a little early. I had a nagging thought, *Could it be my partner? Nicole was still asleep. I quietly pulled on my shorts and running shoes and took off. I ran a little faster this morning thinking about Tone. He did open up a little to me last night. Maybe he is starting to trust me more.* I pushed the thought out of my head. *It just couldn't be Tone. I would know something if it were him.*

As I came into the house, Nicole was starting the coffee. "Good morning," I said, giving her a quick kill. "I have to shower," I said, standing there with sweat pouring off me.

"Yeah, I'll say you do," she said. As I came out of the bathroom, the whole house smelled of bacon. My mouth started to water, and I suddenly felt very hungry. I walked into the kitchen as she was just finishing putting the food on the table. A smile came to her.

"You clean up real nice," she said.

"Thank you, and thank you for being so good to me," I said waving at the table. She looked so sexy in her short and stretched-out T-shirt. It came down just far enough to cover her backside, but when she reached into the cabinets, it raised up to reveal the most perfect behind you will ever see. The neck was stretched out that, whenever she bent slightly, you can see down the front side, and she knew it, so she did a lot of stretching and bending. She knew I was watching.

As she bent slightly in front of me to fill my coffee cup, she said "I think I took very good care of you last night. I'm not so tired this morning, how about it?"

"Most definitely," I said. "You keep teasing me like this, I will have to clear the table."

Well, we can eat first," she said as she pulled her shirt off and sat down to eat.

"Best breakfast I had in a while," I said.

I was an hour late getting to work. Tone was sitting and going through some papers. I noticed both interview rooms were in use. "What's up?" I said.

"Gary and Lucy are following up on the powder that was found. What happen to you? Are you okay?" Tone asked.

"Yeah, I slept through the alarm, that's all," I said.

"Joe, I just want you to know I was thinking about what you said, and I am going to call the therapist in Ellenville. I heard she is pretty good."

"That's good," I said, "what made you decide?"

"Well," he said, "I think it's time to come to grip with my childhood and try to get past it. It's not that I think I am old. It's just I am getting older, and I need to put it behind me so I can move on. I think it may be why I don't have any luck finding the woman that I need. I am just tired of being alone."

I thought to myself, *I knew it couldn't be him, he is just having trouble getting past the past, and he is not gay.*

Lucy came out with Natasha Brown's ex-husband. "Well, thank you for coming in again."

"Anytime," he said, "I would do anything I can to help you find the person responsible."

"Thank you," Lucy said, "if I have any more questions, I'll be in touch."

"You're welcome," he said, "have a nice day."

"You too," Lucy said. After he left, Lucy sat down and said that according to her ex-husband, Natasha sometimes used body powder after a shower, and sometimes she didn't.

"What does that mean?" Tone asked.

"Well," Lucy said, "according to him, she only used the powder when she got her period." Tone went to her file and looked at the crime scene photos.

"Well, I don't see any kind of pads. Let's look at the inventory list. Nope, not there either."

"Check the ME report. See if maybe there was a tampon listed," Lucy told Tone.

He went through and found the report. "Nope nothing," he said. "I guess we can rule it out on Natasha."

Just then, Gary came out with Mary Spiel's ex-boyfriend. "She doesn't use baby powder, that he can remember."

"All right," I said. "Natasha was ruled out. I think we might be able to rule Mary out. Let's just ask a few close friends if they ever saw powder in her bedroom and do the same with Maria."

"We're on it," Lucy and Gary said. They went to the files to get names and numbers.

Just then, John came in. "Hey, guys."

"Hi, John," everyone said.

"What's up?" Joe asked.

"Just stopped by to see how things are going."

"It's a hard one, John, but I'm sure we'll figure it out. John, just for the heck of it, who was it that forgot about the powder?"

"Joe, it was an honest mistake. I don't see any reason for a reprimand."

"I know, John, I'm not getting anyone in trouble. I just want to know for my own mind."

"If I tell you, Joe, you have to swear it won't go further than you."

"I swear, John. I'm not looking to get anyone in trouble."

"Okay, it was Natalie, and if I hear anything, I will never bother with you again. I'm serious about this, Joe."

"We already discussed it, and I'm satisfied it was just an honest mistake."

"Okay."

"John, relax. You won't hear anything."

"Good, now what's going on? Anything new?" I wanted to tell him my mind had been going crazy thinking it might be someone in the department or someone close.

"No, nothing new," I said. "We interviewed a couple of people, and I think the powder might be from a glove, but as far as I know, there weren't any gloves or parts from a glove found at the scene, were there?"

"No. After the powder incident, we at the lab had a meeting, and we all double-checked everything, and there is absolutely nothing there that you don't already have."

"Good, now are you hungry?"

"Now that you mention it, yes, I am."

"Tone, you hungry? You want to go with me and John?"

"Sure, why not," Tone said.

"Last one in the car pays the check." We all ran out. "John pays. Don't worry, I'll leave the tip," I said.

"Oh, thanks a lot," John said. Over dinner, we talked about everything but the case. It's been a while since I've been out with the guys. I would have stayed late tonight, but I already told Nichole I would be over tonight. I told Tone to call Leah since it was kind of early. He said he might just do that.

Yeah, we'll see, I thought. Tone and I gave John ten dollars because he was paying.

I dropped them off at the station and called Nicole to see if she needed something. There was no answer at her house, and her cell went right to voice mail. *She's probably in the shower*, I thought. She knew I was coming tonight. Nicole was just pulling in when I got there. She didn't see me right away. She popped her trunk. When she got out of the car, she saw me pull into her driveway. She looked almost nervous, then she shut her trunk without opening it.

"Need something out of the trunk," I said.

"No, I forgot I put the bag in the back seat. I went to the store and picked up a few things. I thought you would be a little late, so I went and got some things for snacks later and breakfast. Here," she said giving me the bag. "I carried it to the car, you bring it in."

"That seems fair," I said. As she was putting stuff away, I noticed a little blood on her uniform. I asked her if she cut herself. *She looked down and noticed it. She was acting kind of weird tonight,* I thought.

"No," she said, "one of the patients had a bad nosebleed. That's why I was late getting out of work."

"Are they all right?" I asked.

She looked at me like a doe in the headlights. "She, I mean he, is going to be fine."

"Is everything all right?" I asked.

"Fine, why are you asking?"

"I don't know. You seem a little nervous."

"No, I am fine. I want to get in the shower and get the work stuff off me. Care to join me?" she asked as she slipped her pants down.

"There's nothing else I'd rather do," I said. We fooled around a while in the shower, then moved into the bedroom. *She was amazing,* I thought as I was holding her afterward. There was something different tonight. Whatever it was, I liked it.

She got up and poured some wine, and I put some pepperoni, cheese, and crackers on a plate, and we sat in the living room. "Any leads yet?" she asked.

"No, not yet. We do have something new to look at." I told her about the powder and how we interviewed people, and I thought it might be from a glove.

"You mean a surgical glove?" she asked.

"Yes, I think so." She was fighting with the crackers and asked who might have surgical gloves besides someone in the medical field.

"Well," I said, "there are many different types. They sell them in any supermarket with and without powder. So, about anyone could have them. Enough with my work. Are you sure nothing is bothering you?"

"It's nothing," she said, "just a bad day, that's all."

"Anything I can do?"

"No. I will be fine. You ever have a day when you just didn't think you are doing anything right, and you just want to go home and do nothing, but you can't?"

"Yeah, I had plenty of days like that."

"Well, then you know I'll be fine in a bit."

"Okay," I said, "how about some TV?" I turned on a comedy series. After a few minutes, she was cheering up.

"That's my girl," I said as I kissed her on her head. We watched a little more TV, and as we were going into bed, my phone rang. If I didn't have to answer, I wouldn't, but I knew I had to.

"Mecelli?"

"Yeah, where, I'll be right there. We have another one," I said to Nicole.

"I understand," she said nervously.

"I'll call you in the morning," I said as I got my keys and walked out. On the way to the scene, I couldn't help but think about the murders happening when I stayed at Nicole's. Could it be a sign that we should not be together, or does someone not want us together? I did a little digging with Natalie from the lab. She seemed like a straight-up honest woman. There was nothing to believe she had any intent to leave out the fact about the powder. I believe it was an honest mistake.

I pulled up to the scene, the old Ellenville dump in the Berme Road. There were a few officers, and Detective Ed Lackob came over.

"What do we have?" I asked.

"Are you Detective Joe Mecelli?" he asked.

"Yea.,"

"I'm Ed Lackob, nice to meet you."

"Nice to meet you too," I said shaking his hand.

"Well, a few teens were here playing tennis." I looked around, there was a tennis court and a basketball court down the hill a little bit. "The one teen started messing around and hit the ball like a baseball. When they came up looking for the ball, they spotted her." I looked down on the nude female with the clown-like face and blood in the groin area. You can tell she was a very pretty girl with a nice body. *A shame*, I thought. The clothes were stacked neatly in a pile, but her purse was not on top where the rest were.

"Ed?"

"Yeah."

"Are all the kids here that found the body?"

"I believe they are all here, why?"

"I'm not sure, but her purse is not where the rest of the women's were."

"I'll find out if they are all here."

"Thanks, Ed." Just then, Peter pulled up.

"Hey, Joe. How have you been?"

"I've been good, Peter, and you?"

"Kind of busy. What do you say we go out sometime?"

"Yes, I was just thinking that last night or earlier I mean. Look, here comes John, now we can set things up. What about Tone?" I asked.

"Well, he seems kind of weird, but he's your partner."

"What do you mean weird?"

"Well, just like he doesn't know how to have a good time. He's too quiet and to himself.

"Yeah, he's a little shy, but I'm getting through, I think. What's up John?"

"Hey, Joe, hi, Peter. Put a few beers here, and I'll be good."

"I was just thinking, Joe, it's been a while since we been out," Peter said.

"Yes, it has," John said. "Before we leave this scene, we gotta have something set up." Peter and I agreed.

"Okay," I said, "let's get to work." Peter went over the body. "Looks the same," he said. He put the bags over her hands and put her in the bag. John came over.

"Where's Tone?" he asked.

"I don't know," I said.

"Probably running late," Peter said.

"How about seven at our usual?"

"Okay, that's settled." Peter left as Tone pulled in.

"Where the hell you been, Tone?" I asked.

"I did like you said. I called Leah, and we hooked up at her place in Tillson. I got here as soon as I could."

"Good, how was your night then?" I asked.

"It was good, but I will tell you about it later, when we are done here."

"Yeah, right," I said. "Well, anyway, the body is the same, the clothes are the same, but the purse I believe was moved."

"What do you mean moved?" John asked.

"I'm not sure, but in the other scenes, the purse was placed on top of the clothes. If you notice, her purse was just thrown down next to it."

"Do you think it's another copycat?" Tone asked.

"No," I said, "I think it's the same killer, but when the teens found her, I believe one of them went through her purse."

"Well, now that Peter is done, let's check it out," John said. He went to the purse and found her wallet: license, credit cards, and pictures, but not a single dollar.

"I have Detective Lackob looking into the names of the teens. He can deal with the theft," I said.

"Let me see the wallet," I said. I flipped through the pictures and went to the license. Candice Theresa Malone, twenty-four years old, lives on Nevins Street. I gave John the wallet back, and the thought came back to me about the gloves. Everyone on the scene was wearing them, even Tone and me.

"John, the powder that was found on the bodies. Do you think it could have come from one of us here at the scene?"

"Well, the only one here that touches the body is Peter and me, guess we can't rule it out."

I went to find Detective Lackob.

"Ed," I said, "we went through the purse, and everything is right there, except money. Do you think one of the teens went through the purse and took her money? That's what it's looking like. I'm sure she must have been carrying some sort of cash."

"Yeah, who walks around without any money," Ed said.

"Well, that's your case," I said. "If I find out how much she might have had, I will let you know."

"Yeah, thanks," Ed said, "let me figure this out. I'll be in touch."

I went over to Tone. "Well," I said.

"Same scene," he said.

"No tire marks, no footprints, no trace anywhere around the site. I'm sure they won't find any prints of the knife or lipstick."

"You never know," I said. "We may get lucky."

"Yeah, I hope so," Tone said.

"By the way, are we meeting up at seven o'clock, you coming?"

"I think I can make it," Tone said.

"Okay, good. Looks like we're done here. Let's get to the shop and get to work."

"I'll meet you there. I'm going to stop and get a sandwich, you want something?" Tone asked.

"Yeah, get me a bacon, egg, and cheese."

"Okay, I'll see you there."

I went in, turned the lights on, started the coffee, and started a file on Candace when Tone came in. "I got you some home fries too."

"Good," I said. I am hungrier than I thought. I moved the papers aside and started eating. "So how was your date last night?" I asked Tone.

"Well, what there was of it was nice. I didn't get there until about 8:30."

"Why so late? You didn't call right away, did you?" I asked.

"No, I went home and cleaned up a little, and then I showered, then I called around 7:00. We went to this bar and grill in Tillson and had dinner, then went to her place. We talked about school, then she asked if I was on the case around Ellenville. We talked a little about it, without telling her a lot."

"Good," I said. "So, I guess you feel good about Leah?"

"Yes, I think I do. I feel comfortable when I'm with her. I have never felt this way before."

"That's good," I said. "You will feel a lot of things you never felt before."

"I kind of wanted to wait until we catch this person before I started any kind of relationship."

"Why?"

"I don't know."

Probably wanted to have more time to start a relationship, I thought.

Gary and Lucy walked in. "I hear we have another one," Gary said.

"Yeah, I was going to call you guys, but I figured there wouldn't be much there, so I let you guys sleep."

"I got a feeling we are gonna pay for your sleep." I just smiled.

"Well, what do we have?" Gary asked.

"Her name is Candice Theresa Malone, white female, twenty-four years old. She lived on Nevins St. Here is her address. Tone and I will go to her workplace."

"Did you find anything at the scene?" Lucy asked.

"No, it's the same as usual, knife and lipstick. The only difference, I think, is that one or more of the kids that found her went through her purse and took her money."

"What kind of person would go through a dead woman's purse?" Lucy asked.

"I guess a kid would," Tone said.

"Where are the kids that found her?" Gary asked.

"I let the Ellenville Police take care of them. We have too much pressure on us to straighten all of that out."

"Yeah, I guess you're right," Lucy said.

"All right, we ready to work?"

"Let's go," Gary said.

"See you guys later," I said.

"Good luck," Tone said. We all knew we needed all the luck we could get right now.

We had six unsolved murder and not one bit of evidence. We were about to walk out when Alex Fillmore from the DA's office walked in. "Joe, do you have a minute? Hey, guys. How is everyone this morning," he said to Tone, Gary, and Lucy, shaking everyone's hands.

"Sure, that's about all I have right now though. We got another one last night."

"I know," Alex said. "I heard. I'll be quick. Mr. Freeman did not accept our offer. I guess he wants to try his luck at trial."

"How can he try his luck? The evidence is rock solid. There is no way he can win," I said.

"Well, they wanted a speedy trial, so I had to set one up for next Wednesday," Alex said.

"Well, don't worry, Alex, just fax us what we need, and we'll be there. I'm going to see John and Peter later, and I'll let them know to get ready," I said.

"Thanks, Joe, I knew I could count on you," he said with a really big belly laugh. "I'll have everything ready to you, and I'll get back to you on Monday or Tuesday."

"Good, we will be ready," I said as I was walking him to the door.

"And, Joe, good luck with this guy. I hope you get him before he gets another one," Alex said.

"Yeah, I hope too, Alex, have a nice weekend," I said.

"Yeah, if you think getting ready for trial is nice, I will," he said.

"I know what you mean, Alex."

"Tone, nice seeing you again." He shook his hand.

"Yeah, you too, Alex." We all got in our cars and left.

"We going to the insurance office?" Tone asked.

"Yeah, they slept all night. They can go to her home and notify the husband or parents." We drove to the office in quiet.

"Hi, can I help you?"

"Yes, I am Detective Joe Mecelli, and this is Detective Anthony LaFonte. We are here about Candice Malone."

"She is not in today, is she in some kind of trouble?"

"No, ma'am," I said. "I'm sorry to tell you we found her last night."

"Oh my god," she screamed.

Two other women ran out from the back office. "What is it? What's going on?" they asked.

"Candice is dead," the first woman screamed.

They both gasped, "What happened?"

"We found her last night," Tone said. "We are trying to figure out what happened. Can you tell us what type of person Candice was?" Tone asked as he was pouring three drinks of water from the cooler.

"She is a very nice person. The kind of person to give you the shirt off her back. Who would do such a thing to her?"

"We don't know, ma'am. We would like to go through her desk if you don't mind."

"If it will help, it's right here." We looked at the desk, very neat, clean, and everything in its place.

I looked at Tone and gave him a nod. "Ladies," Tone said, "let's go in the back. I have a few questions while my partner has a look around." Once they were in the back, I sat at the desk and looked at her calendar. It had birthdays, holidays, vacations—nothing we could use. After going through her desk, I found nothing to help. Tone got nowhere in the questioning, so we left.

Back at the station, we went over the board and made notes that we had. We really didn't have a lot to go on. Tone made an excuse to leave, so I straightened up and was to leave when Nicole walked in.

"I was just about to go," I said when she went across the room to the board.

"You shouldn't be looking at that," I said as I turned it around.

She said, "Did you look at the names?"

"What about them?"

"Their middle initials spell your partner's name," she said. I looked at the names more closely. There it was, LaFont without the *E*. Hopefully, we can prevent the *E* from happening. I went to my cart with what little I had.

"Do you think he is being set up or is he the one?"

"I don't know," I said. How do we proceed? We talked about different options. We have to bring it to his attention, question him, so to speak. The feeling I had that someone close was involved. How he came in late a couple of times. How it seemed like he was hiding something. Could it be a cry for help?

I went to his apartment. He had clippings from the newspapers all over the table. He had a folder, and I was about to grab it when he stopped me.

"I don't think you want to look at that," he said.

"What are you hiding?" I asked. He broke down, and it all came out: How he had a gut feeling about Nicole not being who she seemed. How he did a background check into her. He found out she was her mother's twin sister, Lisa, and how Lisa never bothered with her and her dad after her mom left. She blamed him for the whole thing. I couldn't help but think he was trying to say he was being set up by Nicole. He noticed his name in all the women's names and tried to figure it out before anyone else did. He said, "You have to help me," and went on to say he was investigating Nicole on his own. He gave me the folder.

As I read all the papers, I thought about all the times she asked about the case, how every time I was in her place I was called out, and how she popped her trunk when I pulled in and shut it without opening it. I was getting a bad feeling after reading all the evidence.

Tone and I went to Nicole's place. We talked for a little bit, and she asked about the case. We talked about how our theory was that someone close was committing these murders in an effort to set up Tone. She changed her tone slightly when we told her that. "But the evidence points to him," she explained. Just then, there was a knock on the door. It was Officer Jankel. He had a search warrant for Nicole's home and car. She seemed confused.

"What is going on?" she asked.

"You don't think I had anything to do with this. Joe, it's me. I can't believe."

"I'm sorry," I said, "we have to check every possible lead."

"So, is that what I become, a lead?"

"I'm sorry." The only things they took from the house were her scrubs from work.

"Okay, let's check the car."

Nicole started screaming, "You can't check my car. You don't have the right." When we opened the trunk, there was a small duffle bag; in the bag were a couple of scalpels, lipstick, a box of gloves, and a .9mm handgun. "That bag is not mine," she screamed. "I don't know how it got there." After collecting the bag and its contents, we booked Nicole for six murders.

Back at the station, she pleaded, "Joe, you got to believe me. I didn't do this, and I don't know where that bag came from."

"What is your real name?" I asked.

She hung her head. "Lisa," she said quietly.

"Why did you change your name? What do you have to hide if you didn't do this?"

"Why would I kill six women and try to pin it on my nephew."

"Your nephew?" I asked.

"Yes," she said.

Just then, Tone walked in. "Everything all right?" he asked. I assured him everything was fine.

"Don't go believing her just because you have feelings."

"No, I just want a few minutes alone." As he left, I turned to her. "You got some explaining to do." She explained how her sister suffered from postpartum depression and could not take care of the baby and how her sister was never the same. She also explained how she started seeing me to see ways to get back at him for making her sister the way she was, but then she realized it wasn't him, he was a nice young man. She could not stop seeing me for she fell in love.

"You've got to believe me, Joe. I didn't do this." They led her away to jail. I just sat there, thinking.

*It had to be he*r, I thought. We didn't have much, but what we had pointed to her. I took a much-needed day off.

The next day, I had to go to John at the CSI lab.

"Hello, John."

"Hi, Joe. Congrats on the arrest. I'm sure it was not easy."

"No, it wasn't. Do you have all the reports ready?"

"Yes, I do," he said. "There was no trace and no blood from any of the victims anywhere in the house or in the car."

"How about the bag?" I asked. "Anything on or in that?"

"No, it was clean, no fingerprints either." I left there and went to my favorite spot to think.

As I looked at the views at the lookout on 52, it all rushed in. After about two hours, it came to me I made the call. We found Tone a few hours later. He was at the local bar. I walked in with two state troopers. He looked at me, downed his drink, and said, "You figured it out." He went without a word. Back at the station, he let it all out: How as a kid he missed his mother and his aunt took her away and how he hated her. He hadn't seen her in over thirty years. When he saw her in town, he decided she had to pay. He thought he could get her convicted when it was him who actually did it. He made a full confession on how he chose the women and why he killed them the way he did. It was his mother's favorite lipstick shade.

I picked Nicole up at the jail. She was very happy I believed in her.

CPSIA information can be obtained
at www.ICGtesting.com
Printed in the USA
LVHW020819130421
684340LV00009B/391